WHO'S THE TARGET?

Abby had good reason to believe she was the target. Three people wanted her dead—three people whom she could identify as her parents' murderers. But one or two things didn't add up, and she decided that maybe Jason could have been the target. She tried to warn him, but he wasn't convinced. Then Abby was attacked in the old ruins of the Bishop's Palace, and she began to wonder if she could be wrong after all. Someone did want her dead—but who?

MARGARET CARR

WHO'S THE TARGET?

Complete and Unabridged

LINFORD
Leicester

First published in Great Britain in 1974 by
Robert Hale Ltd.,
London

First Linford Mystery Edition
published January 1988

Copyright © 1974 by Margaret Carr
All rights reserved

British Library CIP Data

Carr, Margaret
　Who's the target?—Large print ed.—
Linford mystery library
I. Title
823'.914[F]　　　PR6053.A694/

ISBN 0-7089-6500-8

Published by
F. A. Thorpe (Publishing) Ltd.
Anstey, Leicestershire
Set by Rowland Phototypesetting Ltd.
Bury St. Edmunds, Suffolk
Printed and bound in Great Britain by
T. J. Press (Padstow) Ltd., Padstow, Cornwall

The characters in the book are entirely imaginary and bear no relation to any living person

1

SHE stood at the farm gates, a small somewhat forlorn figure, despite the determined smile she forced on her lips as she waved goodbye to the Stewarts. They'd been so kind—picking her up at the hospital, driving her all the way down from the North, stopping for innumerable coffees and a magnificent lunch. But kindness was suspect. There'd been so much of it, masking the pity and the curiosity. People hungering for sensation, thriving on second-hand thrills like bloated jungle leeches, nourishing a relish for the details to embellish and season with all the blood and horror of a Hammer film.

It was bad enough without re-living it for other people's gratification. The quiet evening at home suddenly turned into a horrific nightmare. Three hopped-up youths in search of fresh kicks, brutal, vicious and utterly without mercy. They had killed her parents, they thought they had killed her too, and fired the house to cover up their crime. But she had survived, returning to consciousness to find flames licking at the mutilated bodies of her parents. Nothing on earth could make her forget that night, but talk about it . . . no. She had learned what ghouls people could be. She could recognize the signs. Mrs. Stewart had tried hard but she was like all the others. She wanted to know more. It wasn't every day they gave a lift to someone who had been involved in such a sensational murder.

She sighed and gave one last wave as the Stewarts' car turned the bend. They'd not wanted to leave her. They thought John Wainwright was crazy offering her the use of his cottage. She could have gone to stay with him and had all the comforts of a good home served by an excellent housekeeper. And been within easy reach of the hospital—just in case. Or there were convalescent homes, secluded, peaceful, in beautiful surroundings. The doctors had pressed for that too. She'd had a bad time; fractured skull, broken bones, first degree burns. She was fit enough to leave hospital. They admitted that—they needed her bed—but to go and look after herself, and in an isolated cottage; primitive conditions, no one within call. She had listened unmoved by the sense of what they said. She had changed, only she knew how much. The sensible way, the right and proper way, the way other people thought and acted, governed by convention and man-made laws. It wasn't her way any longer. She was opting out of normal society.

She picked up the small suitcase John Wainwright had bought for her. She had had to fight to get her way. He had been as horrified as the doctors when she had announced her intention of going off on her own but at least he had the vision to see how much she had grown to hate the busy ward with its gossiping patients. A convalescent home would have been much the same. People staring, talking about her, worse . . . trying to get her to talk.

She couldn't take it any longer. And she wouldn't stay with John Wainwright, tempting though he made it sound. Employer, friend, and during this last year a substitute parent, John Wainwright was the only person she had left in the world to love. No, she couldn't stay with him.

The suitcase began to feel like a ton weight. She changed it over to her left hand and quickened her pace. It felt strange to be out on her own, strange, and a little frightening. She hadn't reckoned on this weakness in her limbs. Her legs felt like cotton wool and her arms were aching with the effort of carrying the case. Such a little case too, with hardly anything in it. One of the nurses had bought some essentials for her and she had added a few more herself. A year ago she could have carried it with two fingers.

She stumbled on the rutted track. She was catching up on a herd of cows heading stolidly for a milking shed. A gum-booted farm worker glanced back at her curiously. She looked away from him quickly and studied the farm house. It was a snug, low building, well built and sturdy, but there were tiles missing from the roof and the paint was faded and blistered. A strip of garden separated it from the yard where some brown hens scratched intently in the ground.

She pushed open the little gate and walked up the paved path to the porch, setting the case down with a sigh of relief. Her hands were shaking and her chest felt tight. Had she made a mistake? Should she have made sure she was fit enough before sticking her neck out? The answer was yes, of course, but it was too late now. There was no turning back.

She raised her hand and knocked firmly on the door.

Mrs. Lloyd had been appointed as a watch dog to guard her interests. John Wainwright might have allowed Abby to have the cottage but he'd laid down conditions. She was to carry no heavy shopping, do the minimum of cleaning, no laundry, and at the first sign of a set back was to return at once. He was quite confident Mrs. Lloyd would see the conditions were carried out. She was a good woman, he'd told Abby.

She had lived on the farm all her life, holding on to it through a lot of hard times. Her husband had left her, she'd had a daughter to raise and labour was scarce but she'd struggled on, eking out her income by taking in summer guests.

John Wainwright had first taken his wife to the quiet loveliness of St. David's after she'd had a bad miscarriage. She had thrived in the pure air and beautiful surroundings and later in the year they had brought the boys down for a holiday and stayed with Mrs. Lloyd while they looked for a house to buy as a holiday retreat. Mrs. Lloyd had suggested the cottage. It had been empty for years and needed a lot doing to it but it was cheap, a necessary factor when medical bills for Mrs. Wainwright swallowed a major portion of their income. She never recovered her health completely and her determination to give her husband a daughter finally terminated her life when her younger son, Jason, was only ten years old.

They had continued to spend all their holidays at the cottage. The boys liked it and wouldn't even consider going anywhere else. Mrs. Lloyd kept it in good order in their absence and did what she could when they were down. It had gone on like that for years. She had seen the boys grow up. They had continued to use the cottage, bringing their friends down occasionally when John Wainwright began to find the journey too much for him. The last summer he'd spent at the cottage had been five years ago. Glynis had been around then but she'd always been around. He'd seen nothing that would give him warning. She was Mrs. Lloyd's daughter, a young girl still at school. He'd been totally unprepared two years later for the shock of his eldest son bringing her home with the news that they were married.

Had Mrs. Lloyd received the same shock? Abby doubted it. She'd been on the spot. She must have seen it coming. And she'd said nothing. Gerrard was a good catch of course. John Wainwright had become a wealthy man and his health was not good. A year after the marriage he'd had a severe coronary attack. Glynis had scarcely tried to hide her disappointment at his recovery.

Abby detested her.

And she was prepared to dislike her mother too but the woman who answered the door bore no resemblance to the cool and elegant, beautiful Glynis.

She was big and solid with greying hair and sombre dark eyes. Her dress was drab, its original colour faded with repeated washings. There were lines on her face, deep gouged bitter lines of pain and sorrow. Her hands were red and calloused; hard, capable hands as large as a man's. She was wiping them on a dirty tea towel. "You're Abigail Burton," she said. Her voice was harsh with only a hint of her Welsh ancestry.

Abigail Burton. An old-fashioned name for an old-fashioned girl. The nurses had laughed at it, shortening it to the Abby she had grown to prefer, but John Wainwright would never adopt it. A given name was a given name. It was an insult to her parents to abbreviate it. "You're Mrs. Lloyd?" she questioned doubtfully.

The woman nodded and went on nodding, a curiously blank expression masking her face. Then she shook herself, as if at a shiver, and stepped back quickly. "You've to ring Mr. Wainwright at once. He sounded upset."

She stepped straight to the telephone on a scratched and badly marked desk littered with papers and got the number for Abby, saying briefly, "She's here," before handing the receiver over to her.

He *was* upset. Disjointed phrases leapt to her ear drums bouncing resonantly with some considerable force. She held the receiver away and waited for him to run down without saying a word. He'd seen the papers. A pity. She'd banked on his austere tastes keeping him in ignorance of the statement she'd made to the press. The *Guardian* and *Times* were above reporting on the doings of Abigail Burton, however much the other papers wanted to have a story. Well, she'd had her say and now John Wainwright was having his ... with a vengeance. Behaving in a thoroughly irresponsible fashion ... asking for trouble ... someone could have followed her ... someone might find out where she was staying ... She was all alone ... She had to return at once. The police had been on to him. What was this clue she said she had? What was this about finding her parents' killers? Did she realize she had practically issued an invitation to them to find her before she found them?

There was an ominous silence at that. He was waiting for an answer at last.

"You're making a great big fuss about nothing," she said soothingly. "So I said a few things. They expected me to say just that. What else could I say? I forgive them? I'm going to forget all about it?"

"You've got to forget it. You won't be able to live if you keep on remembering, keep on hoping that they'll be caught. If the police couldn't get them, you won't have a chance. What do you think you're going to do?"

"I'm going to relax and have a lovely time down here—that's all. I've nothing else in mind."

"But the papers . . ."

"Really! Since when did you take any notice of what the papers say? Forget it. They mustn't have had anything better to print."

"At least they didn't get a photograph," he said morosely. "No one will recognize you as you are today."

She didn't disillusion him. There'd been someone waiting with a camera as she'd left the hospital that morning. She'd given her destination too. There'd be ructions when he found that out. She'd have to ring Mrs. McDonald, his housekeeper, and make sure she managed to keep him from finding out. Yes, that was best. She should have done that before. Damn the police. Why did they have to go and bother him? They knew he was a sick man. She'd not blamed them for their failure to get anywhere. They'd had nothing to go on. Only her memory. And that hadn't been functioning too well for weeks afterwards. The photographs she studied ... The questions she'd answered ... They'd done their best. She'd given them credit for that. They shouldn't blame her for lying a little. All she wanted was a chance to get at her parents' killers. A chance. Forget, he'd said. As if she could. The thoughts of what she would do to them had been the only thing to keep her hanging on, fighting for her life. It was all she had to live for.

"Come back," he said. "Stay with me. You'd be far better off here."

"We've been all through that," she said gently. "When I feel better. Right now, I have to be on my own."

"You've not really got some fool plan in your mind of staking yourself out like a goat." He was pleading for reassurance.

She managed to laugh. Phone Mrs. McDonald immediately. Better still, telegraph. There'd be no chance of him overhearing anything then. "Staking myself out! Where do you get your ideas from? Do you think I could face anything like a repetition of that nightmare again? I'd be terrified. Now you know I would."

He did—and she was. There was no doubt about that.

"I'll tell you what I'll do," she said. "I'll phone you every day. Now you forget about your worries. You'll have people thinking you're getting neurotic about me. I'm fine and I'm going to stay fine and I'm going to have a blissful time in your cottage."

He was calmer when she put the phone down, but not wholly convinced. He knew her too well, that was the trouble. She dialled telegrams and sent one off to Mrs. McDonald warning her to keep the police away and any papers that mentioned her name. That done she stood staring at the phone.

"You'll have some tea," Mrs. Lloyd said behind her. It wasn't a question. Nothing like.

Abby turned. There was a look in Mrs.

Lloyd's eyes that gave her a creepy feeling. She said briskly, "That will be fine."

There was nothing she could put her finger on. Nothing at all. Why then did she look as if she'd read her mind? There was fear there, and apprehension, and an awful dread. She was imagining things she told herself firmly. That was what a guilty conscience did for you.

"Sit down." Mrs. Lloyd callously evicted a huge marmalade cat from a chair in front of the hearth where a few logs were smouldering dully. It snarled its protest and sat opposite Abby, eyeing her malevolently as she sat in the chair. She found herself remembering irrelevantly that it wasn't far from St. David's that a French Army had been sent into retreat by a crowd of Welsh women. In their red cloaks and black conical hats they had put the fear of the devil into the superstitious French. Witches. Not so irrelevant after all. Those dark fathomless eyes. And the cat too. Strewth! What was the matter with her? Her first day out and she was imagining a harmless, middle aged woman as a witch. Witches' cats were black anyway.

She settled back in the chair. The room was dark. Light from the small deepset windows was filtered by curtains of a dull olive green and the big heavy furniture further subdued it. There was an odd smell too. Manure? she wondered uneasily. It wasn't very pleasant.

Mrs. Lloyd brought the tea out in a chipped brown pot, pouring it into beakers. There were scones too, on a cracked plate, spread thickly with butter.

Food had lost its attraction for Abby. She ate now only when necessity drove her. Trying to refuse one proved impossible however. Mrs. Lloyd was insistent.

"You've known Mr. Wainwright a long time?" she asked sitting down opposite.

"Since I left school."

"He's very concerned about you."

"I'm one of his lame dogs. He's a very kind man. Well, you know that of course. You've known him much longer." The cat had jumped up on the arm of Mrs.

Lloyd's chair and sat at her elbow like a still, graven statue. She bit into the scone. It was surprisingly good but she almost choked on it when Mrs. Lloyd said, "Why are you not afraid?"

"Should I be?"

"I see death reaching out to put his fingers on you."

The scone suddenly wasn't so good. It tasted like sawdust and ashes. She put it down on the plate Mrs. Lloyd had deposited in the hearth and placed her tea beside it.

It was just another way of getting at her. Another way of finding out something. People tried all sorts of things to get her talking of that night.

"He's put his fingers on me," she said crisply, "and found they burned too much. Now if you don't mind I'd like to get on to the cottage."

To her surprise Mrs. Lloyd made no protest. She got her coat, a big thick navy duffle, and picking up Abby's case led her through the back of the farm. The cat followed at her heels, its tail forming a loop at its tip that made it look like a waving question mark. Now and again it looked around as if to make sure Abby was still following. She was glad Mrs. Lloyd was carrying her case. The cotton wool feeling had spread to more than her legs.

It was shaming. Mrs. Lloyd strode on as if she were skimming over a pavement, downhill at that. She paused at a stile at the end of the field and saw Abby labouring. Her expression didn't exactly soften but she slowed her pace over the next phase, a winding path through an area covered with ferns and gorse and bracken. Right ahead lay the sea, a stretch of deep blue with the sun glinting on its surface.

She stopped again where the path joined another at the cliff edge. "Caerfai Bay is that way," she said with a wave of her arm. "There's a good beach there and a caravan site just above it. There'll be a lot of people down for the weekend with it being a holiday and all but you won't get so many passing the cottage. They prefer to walk the other way—up to the chapel. Are you fond of walking?"

"I can't say I've done much of it for pleasure," Abby said shortly. Sarcasm she could do without.

"You're a town girl," Mrs. Lloyd said flatly. "You should have stayed in the town, in your own environment with friends at hand."

"Mrs. Lloyd, will you stop it, please? I don't know if you think you're doing Mr. Wainwright a favour by making me feel I'm not wanted here but it's not going to work. I'm staying."

"You think I am making this up. You think I want you to go away only because Mr. Wainwright wants you with him. It is not so. I saw death with you, I feel it now cold and dark, filling me with dread."

"I'm scared," Abby said lightly. "Absolutely rigid."

"You laugh," Mrs. Lloyd said. "But later . . ." She shook her head. "I don't think you will laugh then. You will remember my words and you will be sorry." She turned abruptly and began to walk along the cliff path at a rate that soon had Abby gasping for breath again. So she'd be sorry, would she? Heck, she was sorry now. Sorry for the pride that kept her right on Mrs. Lloyd's heels. Left to pick her own way she'd have been going at a snail's pace. There was a damned dangerous drop at one side. At places it needed only a slip and a stumble and eternity would lie ahead. Huge slabs of rock slanted down at acute angles, jutting buttresses of dull red and precipitous slate grey, covered in places by mammoth-sized daisies growing in such profusion from nooks and crannies in the rocks that they looked like a series of cascading flowery carpets.

The path wound around the cliff edge, going up and then down again. After a long pull up a particularly steep rise Mrs. Lloyd stopped. "There's the cottage," she said.

It lay snuggled at the base of a narrow little valley about twenty-five yards from the path. A stream curled down in front of it, passing smoothly under a wooden bridge and tumbling down a steep incline to the sea. There was a beach, a tiny triangle protected by the high shoulders of the cliff which curved around it lovingly to dwindle and lower itself into broken splinters of rock which stuck out from the sea like fierce pointed needles.

"As you see . . . it's very isolated," Mrs. Lloyd said. "Perhaps you'll change your mind now. If you're set on staying in St. David's I could probably arrange for you to have one of the caravans on the camp site. Or there is a guest house up the lane. They'll make you very comfortable there."

"But I'm sure I'll like it here," Abby said and smiled at her. "It looks delightful."

Mrs. Lloyd turned without another word. A strong woman, used to getting her own way. But not this time. She could talk about death, icy fingers or even grinning skulls until she was blue in the face. It wouldn't make one iota of difference. Because she was right. Abby didn't need telling. Death was close. Very close. She had only to reach in her handbag to hand it out herself.

The cat looked back. She wasn't following. Abby eyed it coldly and set her feet in motion once more. She wasn't particularly fond of cats and this one wasn't going to change her opinion. It was bad enough Mrs. Lloyd reading her mind. Odd that . . . How had she done it?

She shrugged. Easy enough. That phone call, the newspapers. It was simple to add two and two, and of course she would want to do as John Wainwright asked. He had probably told her to do her best to make her return to Manchester. There was nothing supernatural about it. It was just coincidence.

Mrs. Lloyd had reached the cottage and opened the door before Abby had reached the wooden bridge. "There's the key," she said, pointing to a bowl on a small, gate-legged table just behind the door. "Don't lose it. There isn't a spare down here and there's no other way in."

"No back door?" Abby looked around the comfortably furnished room with its big chairs, a polished floor, carelessly scattered rugs and a rough stone fireplace that took up a good half of one wall. It was bigger than she'd expected. An open staircase spiralled up at the side. Through a door at the other end she could see what looked like a modern kitchen; built-in cupboards, brightly painted surfaces, a big stove.

"What for?" Mrs. Lloyd said. "You'll be comfortable enough, without a back entry. I'll take your case up."

She went up the spiral staircase, pausing on the squared landing at the top. "Bathroom, front bedroom and the boys' room." It was the boys' room she entered, dumping the case on the bed at the far side near the window. "This was Gerrard's bed," she said. "It's a long time since he's used it but you'll find it well aired."

It *was* a long time. Three years to be exact. Gerrard hadn't been down to the cottage since his marriage to Glynis; down to St. David's at all for that matter. Glynis's doing of course. No one had been quicker to wipe the mud off her feet. She loved town life. Abby wondered if her mother missed her. Now that she had met her she was all the more convinced that she must have known what was going on in that summer three years ago. Not much would escape those eyes.

"How about Jason's bed?" she said, sitting down on it. "Do you keep that aired too?"

"I keep all the beds aired," Mrs. Lloyd said repressively. "And you'll find a good stock of tinned goods in the cupboards. Not that you'll need them. There's plenty of fresh vegetables and fruit and all the dairy produce you can use. Mr. Wainwright said that was what you needed. Good wholesome foods. There's a casserole in the oven. You'll only have to heat it for a few minutes. I'll get steak for you tomorrow. One of the men will be round every morning. You tell him what you want and I'll bring it round later. Don't thank me," she added as Abby opened her mouth. "I'm being well paid for it."

"Nevertheless, I'm very grateful," Abby said stiffly.

"Are you?" Mrs. Lloyd said with a touch of scepticism. "It strikes me that you're so suspicious of anyone doing you a favour that I wonder what you would think I was up to if I wasn't getting paid for it. If I could make a suggestion . . . No." She turned. "You'll probably think I want this cottage empty to let out to someone else, making some money on the side, safe from interference with Mr. Wainwright so far away."

"That thought has not occurred to me," Abby said with truth, following her down the stairs.

"Why hasn't it? Why aren't you afraid? Why aren't you even a little disconcerted when I tell you what I feel?" The sombre eyes raked her face, making it hard for her to meet them. "Maybe it's because it would take a lot to surprise or disconcert me after what I've been through," she said after a short pause.

"No. It's not that." Mrs. Lloyd sighed. "I don't know what it is. You don't even think I'm a silly old fool, do you? I could understand that. A lot of people have thought it at one time or another. They've usually found out their mistake. Will you promise me something? Come to me if you're in trouble. Don't let pride stand in your way. And another thing." She went into the kitchen and came back with a canister of pepper. "Carry this with you. It's as good a weapon as any for gaining an advantage. Lock all the windows at night. You'll hear if anyone comes up the stairs. They creak." She pressed the pepper into Abby's hand. "Take care. I beg of you."

Abby stood at the door and watched her stride quickly up the cliff path. The cat was right behind her again. She put the pepper in her bag. After all, one never knew. A gun wasn't always the answer.

2

IT was almost seven o'clock. There was time enough to examine her surroundings before the light went. She picked the key out of the bowl and locked the door before continuing up the path to reach the other side of the valley. At places she had to force her way through the gorse which constantly tugged at her clothing. An overgrown path—not many passers-by. It looked as if Mrs. Lloyd had been right.

She retraced her footsteps and went down to the little beach, hopping from one side of the stream to the other to the natural footholds. She'd have to get some more shoes, sandals too. So many things to buy. It was surprising how much one took belongings for granted. Left with absolutely nothing, not even the clothes she'd stood up in, she had a long way to go before everything was replaced. Some things, of course, would never be replaced.

She leaned against one of the thickly encrusted rocks feeling the prick of the limpets through her trousers. Here in this peaceful solitude it was hard to accept the reality of violence. She had been such a dull pudding of a girl. Nothing had ever happened to her. And her parents . . . They'd never done a harmful thing to anyone in their lives. There were nights when she woke up screaming, reliving it in a nightmare that was ten times worse than when it happened, knowing what was to come and being unable to prevent it.

At least she wouldn't wake anyone here, have the night nurse fussing over her and hear the fretful mutters of the other patients wakened so abruptly out of sleep.

She could try to wean herself from the drugs. It felt like an admission of weakness every time she took a pill but a sleepless night was worse than the chance of having a nightmare. At night, in the dark, with so many other people sleeping peacefully in the ward, her thoughts took on macabre turns. The doctors came out with the age-old platitudes of time healing everything, only so far there'd been no dulling of the images, no blunting of the hurt. John Wainwright had hopes of St. David's instilling some of its peace within her. He'd seen what a transformation it had made on his wife so many years before. He'd talked of it, drawing pictures of the scenery, the flowers and the birds. She didn't like to think what she would have done if he'd not been around those months in the hospital. A lame dog, she'd told Mrs. Lloyd. But it was more than that and she knew it. She was more like a daughter to him. Right from the start they had been drawn to each other. The plain Jane with no arts and not much brain and the old-fashioned family solicitor with great charm and understanding and a facility for seeing what lay under the most unprepossessing exterior.

She smiled faintly as she remembered that first meeting. She'd gone for an interview, still in her school uniform, knees knocking, stuttering and stammering and getting the name wrong when the girl at the desk asked her what she wanted.

They'd advertised for a junior. £5 a week. It had seemed a fortune.

The girl had giggled. It had seemed mocking then. She had been ready to turn and flee when Mr. Wainwright had toddled down the corridor and taken in the situation at a glance.

Somehow she'd found herself in his office admitting that she'd failed her "O" levels and tried for other jobs without success. Her parents wanted her to stay on at school but she knew it wouldn't be any good. She didn't have the brains for any kind of scholastic career. "But I'm not stupid," she assured him. "And I can work hard."

He'd sat behind his desk, a spry, little gnome of a man, nodding and twinkling and making her feel so much at ease she forgot the shyness and uncertainty which made her an outcast in the world of bright and confident youth, she forgot that she was fat and plain and that no one thought it worthwhile to take a second glance at her. He made her feel important, a personality instead of a person. As she grew to know him better she discovered that was part of his charm. He could make anyone feel that way, getting away with the most outrageous demands simply because no one could resist doing anything for someone who had such an unaccountably good opinion of them.

Abby slogged away at nightschool for his sake, emerging with certificates to prove she'd reached a reasonably high standard in shorthand and typing and also book-keeping. She became his secretary, pleasing him was her main interest in life. He didn't create when she made a mistake or take her to task for forgetting an appointment. Not like Gerrard. Gerrard expected perfection and showed his displeasure in no small way when he didn't get it. He made her nervous and inevitably she made more mistakes. The time following John Wainwright's attack had been a time of misery and stretched-out nerves. Worry for John Wainwright had been heightened by Gerrard's attitude. He was taking over everything as though his father were never coming back. She'd told herself people recovered from heart attacks, they led a normal life again, but the waiting had seemed an eternity.

He had come back but it was only to potter around and keep his hand in. Now he had retired completely and she knew she couldn't return to work for Gerrard alone, even if she wanted to. He had got a new secretary, he had everything the way he wanted it and he was bringing in a new partner. The firm wouldn't be the same. It had been such a happy place. Passing from father to son for over a century had given it a family relationship that was reflected in the people who worked there. The chief clerks spent their lives at the same desk, the girls stayed on and on until they were married or had babies and the articled clerks served devotedly until they were fully fledged, always remaining if given the chance.

Gerrard had ideas that would change that. He disliked the label of family solicitor. He was modern and progressive. A cold man, totally unlike his father. He had come into the firm, following tradition, when Abby had been twenty-one. He'd married a year later but despite his obsession for Glynis it in no way softened his feelings. If anything he had become even more withdrawn from other people, especially his brother.

Jason was two years younger than Gerrard. He too was unlike his father but he had inherited his father's greatest asset —his charm. He could turn it on like a tap. Abby had seen him in action and despite the certainty that unlike his father he didn't care one whit for other people she couldn't fail to be impressed by the demonstration. After his visit the girls in the office hadn't stopped talking about him for weeks.

He was a problem. He always had been. Polite requests to take him from school had led to instant expulsions from others as he grew older. He'd been in trouble with the police when he was only seventeen and after a period in the navy had gone from one job to another, landing on his father at periodic intervals for help of one kind or another. It was usually for money. He lived expensively; fast cars, gambling, beautiful girls, a luxury flat in London. He had everything he wanted out of life . . . until he met Glynis.

Abby knew about it—as she knew everything that touched on John Wainwright's life.

Gerrard and Jason had never been particularly close. Their difference in temperament was far too marked. Gerrard, bookish and serious, quiet and reserved with a brilliant brain, and Jason, wild and reckless, often foolish, defying authority in any shape or size simply because it was authority.

There was no open breach between them however—not until the summer Glynis grew up.

Jason was the first to fall. He'd been twenty-four then and Glynis was seventeen, very young still, but she knew what she wanted and she only had to look in the mirror to be assured of her chances of getting it. It hadn't taken her long to discover that Jason's extravagant tastes hid a non-existent bank balance and a trail of bad debts and a father who was getting tired of hauling him out of trouble. Gerrard had a future, a place in the firm and he never put a foot wrong where his father was concerned. She married him on her eighteenth birthday.

Jason didn't find out until afterwards and the first opportunity of seeing Gerrard had been at the office on his first day back after the honeymoon. There had been a fight, almost a murder. Jason had half killed Gerrard and then he had walked out, dropping from sight completely. They had had to put an appeal over the radio when his father was so dangerously ill a year later. He had returned to see him and after that kept in touch, arriving at infrequent intervals to stay with his father. John Wainwright derived little pleasure from his visits. There were no longer appeals for money from his son. He threw it around as if he had discovered an unlimited supply from which he could draw.

He began seeing Glynis again too. They had bought a house in Altrincham, not far from John Wainwright's, and Glynis had settled into the social fling with an enthusiasm Gerrard did not share. Jason met her at parties, took her for lunch occasionally and bought her expensive presents.

After John Wainwright's attack and his absence from the office Abby caught up on the news only when she paid him a visit but she always knew when Jason was home. Gerrard gave it away by so many little signs. Phoning Glynis at odd times of the day, fault-finding and flaring into a temper at the slightest thing. Glynis had him just where she wanted him—that was the trouble. He was afraid to tackle her, afraid of losing her, afraid of hearing her admit she was having an affair with Jason. He had to appear to trust her. He had to meet Jason and act as if there was no enmity between them. It was an immense strain on him, especially as Jason took a delight in baiting him. He knew of course exactly what Gerrard suspected.

"He's grown hard and unfeeling," John Wainwright told Abby sadly. "He doesn't care about anyone. He's even cruel." He blamed Glynis for the change in him and there was something else he worried about too. The lavish way Jason threw money around made him suspect he had turned to crime. He didn't seem to have a job, he was unusually reticent about what he did in London and more than once he'd dropped everything at a moment's notice after a phone call from a very odd-sounding man. His passport too, pages filled with entry and exit stamps, and constantly carried with his wallet, almost as if ready for instant flight.

Abby shivered. She didn't want to think about that. If John Wainwright heard his son was on the run it would just about kill him. She reckoned she herself had deducted ten years from his life.

She went back to the cottage and went upstairs to unpack, finding out that the chest of drawers held a motley collection of male clothing; jeans, sweaters, a couple of sports shirts, swimming trunks. It was just as well she had very little to stow away—underclothing, another pair of trousers, two sweaters and a blouse. She put her slippers by the side of the bed, her pyjamas on the top. The room was minimally furnished. There were just the two beds, the chest of drawers and a built-in cupboard that would do service as a wardrobe. It had fishing rods in it and some rope-soled canvas shoes. Too big for her. She tried them.

There was a little more furniture in the front bedroom. A chair, a dressing-table with two cut glass candlesticks on an elaborate lace doily, a wardrobe with a full length mirror. She stared at her reflection curiously. She didn't know herself, this stranger with the big grey eyes and narrow pointed face. Why she actually had bones! Who would have believed it?

She went downstairs and put the kettle on, looked at the casserole and decided it could wait until the next day. She wasn't really hungry and she couldn't be bothered. A cup of tea would do her. She opened all the cupboards. Crockery in one, tinned goods in another, butter, bacon, eggs, cheese, bread. There was enough food to feed a starving family for a week. Vegetables too, stacked in tiered baskets. And wine! And beer! Well, well. Mrs. Lloyd was catering for every taste. Pans under the sink, a cylinder of Calor gas by the stove. Not so primitive after all. Electricity wasn't such a necessity. And that reminded her. The lamps. She should have asked Mrs. Lloyd how they worked. The shadows were lengthening. She didn't want to be caught in the dark.

She fiddled about with them without success and came to the conclusion that they needed oil or whatever what one put into the bases to make them light. Mrs. Lloyd had fallen down on her job unless there was a can in the kitchen somewhere.

She decided to leave it. An explosion she could do without and there were plenty of candles. She went for the glass candlesticks in the bedroom upstairs and fixed candles into them.

Once the sun disappeared over the horizon the night came quickly. It felt colder too. She looked at the fire laid in the hearth. It wasn't worth lighting it now. A pity she hadn't thought of it earlier. It could have been warming the water. She'd have liked a bath but not a cold one. The water felt as if it came fresh from a mountain spring.

She had another cup of tea and put her feet up over the arm of the chair. Supposing it worked? Supposing they did come after her? She hadn't thought it out. Six bullets in the gun. Two for each of them. Supposing she hit them—that was questionable. She'd have to let them get quite close so that it was impossible to miss. Their knee caps—that was a good place. They wouldn't be able to walk again if she shattered them. But then she'd have to go for help. It wouldn't do for them to bleed to death. She didn't want that. No, that was too good for them.

She put her cup down and snuffed out one of the candles. They wouldn't come tonight. No one had followed them down. She'd been disappointed. Maybe they didn't read the papers. There was tomorrow of course. She could hope then.

She locked the door and made sure all the windows were bolted and then took her bag and one of the candles up to bed with her. She'd have a good night's sleep and wake with more strength in the morning.

She undressed and had a quick wash, filling a glass of water and taking it into the bedroom. One pill? Or two? Or maybe none at all? She shouldn't need anything to get her off tonight. She took the two bottles out of her bag, the bigger one for sleep, the smaller one for pain. She had a month's supply. It was something to be grateful for. They didn't consider her a suicidal type or one likely to make a mistake. Sometimes she'd wondered. There were blanks in her memory, not the first ones when she had been so ill, but later when there was no excuse. Days passing without being noticed, words said that she did not remember. It was natural they told her. But it worried her.

She put the bottles down by the glass of water and blew out the candle. She'd have to bring a chair in here, something to put her things on. The floor was no place.

The bed was soft after the hard hospital one. She felt herself sinking into sleep almost at once. No dreams tonight . . . please, no dreams.

She woke suddenly, sweating and rigid with fear. Something had pierced through her sleep, some alien sound. She lay without moving a muscle, her ears straining so hard they almost sprouted antennae.

Mrs. Lloyd was right. The stairs did creak. She heard them most distinctly.

3

STEADY, unhurried footsteps. One person alone. She slid her hand out from under the bedclothes and groped for her handbag. Her fingers fumbled with the catch and then closed tightly around the cold steel of the gun. She waited for the door to open. She needed a torch. He'd have one for sure. He could blind her. She wouldn't be able to aim the gun.

She was out of bed before the thought reached completion, pulling up the covers and roughly straightening them. He'd think the room was empty. There was nothing to give her away. He'd have to cross right to the window and peer over her bed before he could see her things. She lay flat under the bed. The floor was ice cold. It was like lying on a marble slab in a morgue. She clenched her teeth and forbade such thoughts. He was a long time. What was he doing? The flushing of the lavatory answered her and then the door opened and let in a glow of light. He did have a torch. She saw a pair of legs, suede shoes, twill trousers—and the cat—the huge marmalade cat from the farm, its eyes glowing like liquid jewels and staring straight at her.

She stared right back, mesmerized into complete stillness and out of the corner of her eye saw one shoe pulled off and then the other. This was no intruder with murder on his mind. He acted as if he had a perfect right to be there. Who was he? Someone from the farm? But he'd know she was there.

Jason! It had to be Jason. Not Gerrard, not without Glynis.

She opened her mouth but her brain was paralysed. What could she say? There was nothing that wouldn't make her out to be an absolute fool. And then it was too late. The trousers followed the shoes.

She closed her eyes. This was a kind of death. Any minute now he'd wonder what the cat was staring at and take a look.

And if he didn't? She would have to wait until he was asleep and then creep out and go into the front room. Explanations would come better in the morning. She needn't tell him she'd been under the bed.

The torch light shifted and went out with a snap. Her eyes flew open. He'd have put it on the floor. There was nowhere else . . . unless he wanted a lump under his pillow. She held her breath. There was a creak as he got into bed. Above her. That was that then. He'd feel the warmth. He couldn't but help it. She rolled out from under the bed groping for the torch and her hand closed on it a second before his. He reacted as if he'd touched a red hot poker, his breath drawing in sharply.

She fumbled for the switch, awkwardly scrambling to her feet. It was a heavy, rubber-encased torch. No switch. Then she found a knob and pressed it, catching him full face, half out of bed.

It was Jason. There was no mistaking

those hard reckless lines, that jutting nose.

He was frozen in an absolute stillness, and then it seemed as if the whole bed erupted. She went down, the blankets swirling over her and then the beam of the torch was on her face and Jason was saying blankly, "Good God!"

She blinked dazedly, struggling desperately for breath. He was on top of her, his weight pinning her down beneath the blankets he'd flung at her. She'd lost the gun and hit her head. It felt as if the surgeons were back in there, sawing away for dear life.

"Who are you?" he demanded. "What are you doing here?"

"Get—off—me," she said murderously.

"Not before you answer my questions," he said. "That was a gun in your hand."

"So what if it was. I didn't fire it, did I?" She exerted every muscle in an effort to dislodge him and failed lamentably.

He laughed when she gave up with an angry baring of the lips in disgust at her own weakness and taking her completely by surprise, bent his head and kissed her.

For the first few seconds she lay as one stunned. Jason Wainwright kissing her! The very wildest of dreams coming true. She felt the warmth of his body through the blankets, wondered uneasily whether he had on anything at all, and had a momentary vision of the girls in the office. There wasn't one of them who'd fail to give her right hand to change places with her at this moment.

He raised his hand, smiling at the expression of shocked stupefaction on her face. "Anyone would think you'd never been kissed before," he said. "Such outrage!"

She took a deep breath. Somewhere along the way both heart and lungs seemed to have ceased to function. "Do that again," she said dangerously. "Just you try to do that again."

"Anything to oblige." He bent his head and this time she was ready. Her teeth almost met in a satisfying bite at his lower lip.

He swore, jerking back, his hand going to his mouth and she pushed wildly at his chest, struggling to free her hands from the folds of the blanket and then she stopped, suddenly frightened at the expression on his face.

He put the torch down deliberately and slid both his hands around her face, holding it as if in a vice.

"Let's try again," he said softly. "See what you can do this time."

She tasted his blood as his mouth came down hard. Too late she realized his first kiss had been no more than a token peck, given on impulse with no thought or desire behind it. This time he meant business.

Common sense told her to lie limp. To feign death was the only way to turn a rampant lion from his prey but this was not the jungle and while she might have been able to remain perfectly still with a lion sniffing at her heels it was a different matter to lie still when Jason Wainwright was kissing her as if he never meant to stop.

She twisted and squirmed, her heart pounding frantically, her head nearly bursting with the thought of what came next. If only she wasn't pinned down so completely. If only she could get one hand free. She'd twist it around in that thick black hair and yank so hard he'd be lucky if it didn't come out by the roots. She'd scratch his face. She'd . . .

"Had enough?" He raised his head but retained his grip around her face.

He was smiling, mocking and arrogant.

"I am sick to my stomach," she said, trying to sound calm and dignified and wishing she had more breath in her. "Does that answer you?"

"It's one answer. Maybe you can give me a few more. What are you doing here?"

"I might ask you the same question. Your father has lent me this cottage. He didn't imagine you'd be walking in at the dead of night to frighten me out of my wits."

"You know who I am?" He frowned, his thick eyebrows almost meeting.

"I know who you are and what you are," Abby said scornfully. "But for all your faults I didn't imagine you had to descend to force to kiss a girl. Do you think you could allow me to get up or are you going to go on and rape me?"

"Is that what you are hoping for? Sorry. I don't go in for that sort of thing." He picked up the top blanket and smoothly draped it round his waist before he stood up, smiling at her with blandness added to the mockery. "It's no use your staying down there. I won't listen to any pleas. Besides, that floor must be very cold on your back."

"I'm truly surprised you've managed to remain alive so long." She bounced to her feet, regretting her impetuosity immediately as the surgeons got busy with their saws again. For a moment the room spun dizzily. She felt for the edge of the bed and sat down square on the cat which retaliated with a spitting snarl and extended claws, sending her soaring adrenalin count rocketing even further.

"My bed warmer," Jason said, soothing

the cat with his hand, stroking it from his head along the whole length of the sleek, well nourished body.

"Mrs. Lloyd said that was Gerrard's bed," Abby said accusingly.

"And you preferred that to mine? Amazing! Do you know Gerrard too?"

"Of course I know him. Haven't you recognized me yet? You called me a stupid interfering little twit, or words to that effect, last time we met. Just because I threatened to call the police."

He took another look at her, a good look, shining the torch in her face again. "I've never seen you in my life," he said flatly.

"Such conviction! You've met me twice to be exact. The first time was when you had to have five hundred pounds in rather a hurry. A debt of honour you told your father. I suppose some tout or other was chasing you for it. You came to the office and spent an hour beguiling the girls when your father was busy with a client. You even wasted a little of your precious charm on me. Or tried to. I suppose you thought that it would be a good thing to have an ally in your father's secretary. You never know when it might come in useful."

"You were my father's secretary?"

"For six years."

"You're lying. He had an old bat that was with him for years and then he took a fancy to a fat lump of a girl with eyes like granite and a nose that stuck out like a mountain."

It was astonishing how that hurt. She touched her nose tenderly. It hadn't been as big as that, a little bumpy maybe. "I had a new nose," she said stiffly. "The old one got smashed. And if my eyes were like granite it was only when you were around. I hated you for the way you treated your father. He loves you and you don't care. You have never cared. And now he's old and ill you worry him more than you've ever done before." She sat down on the bed—well away from the cat. "Would you mind getting out of here now, and taking your bed warmer with you. I've had a very tiring day."

"I'm not going anywhere. And I want to know what you are doing with a gun."

She blinked. He produced it, handling it with a familiarity that betrayed his acquaintance with a gun. "Fully loaded! But I'm glad to see you left the safety catch on. Would you have fired it?"

"Not at you," she said coldly. "Tempting though it may seem. May I have it back please."

She held out her hand but he ignored it.

"Have you got a licence for it?"

"It's no business of yours."

"So you haven't. Mind you, I would have been very surprised if you had. Where did you get it from?"

One of the nurses had got it for her. An Irish girl with a brother in the IRA. It had cost her £20.

"I bought it," she said shortly.

"It's a funny thing to buy," he said musingly. "Most girls would settle for a poker by the side of the bed if they get nervous." He turned the beam on her again. "You don't *look* the nervous type."

Her hand went up to shield her eyes.

"And you're not Abigail Burton," he added firmly.

"I'm surprised you remembered the name," she said tartly.

"Who could forget Abigail? I thought it suited her perfectly. You now ... You're a Diana or a Sibyl, a—"

"I'm Abigail Burton," she interrupted with a snap. "And if I wanted a discussion on names I'd choose a far better time and place than this to do it in. I want to get back to the bed you've made such a mess of and resume my interrupted sleep. Will you *please* get out and give me back my gun."

"Both requests refused forthwith," he said cheerfully. "There are two beds in here and I'm keeping an eye on you."

"You are not."

"And how do you propose to stop me?"

She eyed him with a stony face. "I am not sleeping in the same room as you."

"What are you afraid of? Losing your virtue? You needn't worry. You keep to your bed and I'll keep to mine."

"That is hardly the point."

"Then what is? Don't tell me you're worried about your reputation? I'm staying the weekend. People will talk whether we share the same room or not. Gerrard will be pleased at that, won't he?"

"Gerrard?" She frowned. "What's he got to do with it?"

"If you are Abigail you should know." He smiled at her as if he'd made a point

Her frown deepened. "Just tell me why I should claim to be Abigail Burton if it were untrue."

"I think I've solved that. You must know her obviously. She could have asked you to come down here and while you're getting free lodgings she could be off with Gerrard, basking safely in the assumption that everyone thinks she's here."

"Off with Gerrard!" Abby exclaimed incredulously. "Are you out of your mind?"

"I have it on very good authority that Gerrard is in love with Abigail Burton."

Abby stared at him with her mouth

open. "Glynis!" she decided. She was the only one. "If you're still believing her lies," she said tersely. "You want your head examining. Why don't you remember the fool she made of you once and wonder what she is up to this time? You'd be far better occupied than trying to dream up motives for me to claim my own name. Why Gerrard's stupid about Glynis! He'd never dream of looking at anyone else."

Jason stared at her with a face absolutely devoid of expression.

"As you won't move out," she went on coldly. "I will. And if you try to follow me I'll split your head in two."

He didn't move a muscle. She went out with a feeling that was almost disappointment.

The big double bed was cold and there was a draught from the window that seemed to come straight from the depths of the sea.

She huddled under the bedclothes getting colder and colder. It was a damp cold too. It seemed to inch through her skin and penetrate through her bones. How long since anyone had slept in this bed? It could have been decades from the way it felt. And she wasn't going to break the record this night. Sleep had never been farther away. Her head began to ache in earnest. She'd have to resort to her pills. And while she was about it she could get her gun back. Jason must be asleep by now.

She got out of bed and crept out of the room. She had her hand on the door of the back room when a flicker of light caught her eye.

She peered over the banisters. Someone was downstairs with a pencil beam torch. The beam travelled around the room and pin-pointed the stairs. A foot was illuminated, a muddy town shoe which had once been well polished. A second came into sight. He was keeping to the very edge of the stairs.

She backed soundlessly into the bedroom where Jason was sleeping and went down on the floor between the beds. He'd put the torch where it had been before but there was no gun with it. She felt all over the floor and then decided that he'd have put it under the pillow whether it was lumpy or not.

The stairs were creaking, but very faintly, not as they had done when Jason walked up.

She slid her hands under the pillow listening to the even tenor of Jason's breathing.

She could wake him up but he would be sure to demand explanations and that would take time. Time for the intruder to hear him and be frightened away.

The steel of the gun met her fingers and with infinite care she started to pull it out, freezing as Jason stirred and then pulling it out like lightning as he lifted his head to turn over.

He settled down again and she had the sensation of someone else holding their breath as she was doing. She strained her eyes towards the door but the darkness was absolute.

She slid the safety catch off and went

down between the two beds on her stomach.

The little beam of the pencil torch stabbed suddenly into the darkness. He stood perfectly still at the doorway conducting a methodical survey before he took another step.

Abby stationed her finger over the button on the heavy torch.

He was taking great pains to be silent; the time between each step seemed an eternity. Her finger on the torch button ached with the suspense of holding back and then before he rounded the base of the first bed a spitting snarl broke the silence and she felt the rush of wind as the cat on Jason's bed launched itself through the air. The man's breath choked in his throat and he jumped back in terror.

Abby's finger came down involuntarily on the torch and she swung it up and high-lighted a chamois leather driving glove and a gun. She saw the trigger finger jerk and flung the torch straight at it, rolling under the bed as the shot rang out, deafening in the small room.

He didn't wait to take a second shot. She didn't think he'd meant to fire the first. He bolted, and jumped down the stairs in huge leaps that from the sound of it brought him to quick grief.

She went after him, straining her eyes in the darkness but he picked himself up well before she got to him and shot towards the door. There was nothing to be seen when she reached it, only the blackness of the night and a faint luminescent sheen from the sea.

She closed the door and something tinkled outside. A key. She felt blindly and managed to retrieve it, locking the door and leaving the key inside the lock. Somewhere she'd read that a door couldn't be unlocked when the key was in the keyhole at the other side. She put the table in front of the door just in case. It didn't do to believe all one read and if he came back again she wanted to hear him. She'd never have heard those soft footfalls if she'd been asleep.

She checked the windows and came back to the door. Unless Jason had left the key in the lock outside it looked as if the intruder had possessed a key of his own.

She shook her head. It didn't add up.

She hadn't seen his face but there was more than an impression of a full-grown man to go by; there were the expensive town shoes, the chamois leather driving gloves, and the fact that he'd been alone. Those three hopped-up youths travelled in the pack, not singly, and they wore dirty ragged jeans and plimsolls. Even with all her imagination she couldn't picture them in a suit. And even if they'd got one of the morning papers hot from the presses they'd never have found the cottage in the dark and just happened to have a key for it.

She went pensively back up the stairs and bumped into Jason coming down.

He grabbed her by the shoulders as she uttered a faint shriek and fell backwards. "What the devil do you think you're playing at?" he demanded angrily.

"Unless you want a bullet in your guts I wouldn't advise you to go creeping about in the dark," she said in a deceptively soft voice. "Have you got your key?"

"Of course I've got my key and I want that gun too. Hand it over."

"Show me the key, Jason."

She didn't do it deliberately. It was merely that in regaining her balance she touched his ribs slightly with the gun.

She pulled it away immediately. After all, the safety catch was still off, but he dropped his hands from her shoulders. "You're not safe to be left loose," he said. "I want some light on the scene." He brushed past her and she followed him slowly.

She was relieved to see he'd taken time to pull on his trousers as the light flared and he lit a candle.

"Your key," she said.

"Persistent, aren't you?" He pulled it out of his pocket and threw it at her. "Want a drink?" There was a zipped airline bag on one of the chairs and he plucked out a bottle of Haig.

"I don't drink," she said primly. "Does anyone want you dead?"

"So far as I know you're the only one." He got a glass and half-filled it, then went to the tap and added a mere splash of water. "What do you want the key for? To lock me out or to lock me in?"

"I only wanted to see it." She put it down on the table. "We had a visitor. He had a key."

"And I suppose it was at him you fired, not me."

"I didn't fire. He did."

"Let me see the gun."

"No." She retreated a few steps. He wouldn't give it back. She knew it. "Don't you believe me?"

"Frankly, no."

"That's your loss then." She turned and went upstairs and lit the candle there, sliding the gun under the mattress of Jason's bed, just in case he decided to search for it when she was asleep. With a bit of luck he might not look there.

Her pill bottles had been disturbed. She wondered if he'd been in her bag too and reached for the glass of water. There was nothing much in it. Cheque book, wallet, medical and hospital card, a biro, a packet of tissues. Oh and the pepper. What would he have thought of that?

She swallowed a pain killer and unscrewed the bottle of sleeping pills, shaking two into her hand. No half measures now. She had to have some sleep.

"What do you take those for?" Jason said from the doorway.

She answered without turning round. "To stop me screaming in the night."

He advanced into the room, the candle flame flickering as he moved. "What were you in hospital for?"

"As if you didn't know! I suppose you want it first hand too, all the bloody details. You people turn my stomach." She stood up, recognizing an extreme reluctance to go back into the front room, into that cold and damp bed.

Jason's face wavered and steadied

before her. She walked around the bed. She wasn't going to make it. The floor rose to meet her, slowly, almost lazily. She put her hands out but they too moved slowly. She couldn't save herself. She couldn't do a thing. She closed her eyes and went down without a murmur.

4

JASON contemplated her inert figure with suspicion. She'd fallen with such graceful abandon he thought it too good to be true. It was only when she remained completely still that he set the candle down and went to her.

She was ice-cold to the touch. He picked her up and put her in bed, piling the blankets on top of her.

She shivered, muttering inaudibly for a second and then relapsing into a frozen stillness again.

He went to the pill bottles and for the second time that night counted their contents. He'd come into contact with neurotics before and was under no illusions. Two gone. She must have had some before she went to bed for them to have knocked her out as quickly as that but she'd obviously not taken an overdose.

He stood frowning down at her. Abigail Burton! It was a hard fact to assimilate. Such a radical change in appearance. But there was her name on the bottles, on the cheques in her cheque book and in her wallet.

He felt her forehead and then put his hand under the bedclothes. She wasn't getting any warmer.

Where was the cat? His bed warmer! He looked around the room and realized he'd not seen it since he'd been so abruptly wakened by its flying exit from his bed. He went to the door and called it with no result and then went downstairs, bumping into the table she'd put before the door. Cursing he unlocked the door, peering into the darkness. No cat. Not a sign. She'd probably frightened it half out of its wits with the noise of that gun.

Well, he had to get her warm somehow. He didn't want a sick girl on his hands. He got into the bed and moulded his body around hers, on the alert in case she came to. There was no sense in taking any chances. She was obviously capable of doing the first thing that came into her head, however violent.

Her body felt very thin and slight. He thought of Glynis, of the difference between them. When Glynis had told him Gerrard has asked for a divorce and the girl was Abigail Burton he'd thought it the biggest joke of the year. It didn't seem so funny now. It was even credible. A man would want to take care of this girl, look after her, cherish her. She needed that kind of love. A man would feel strong and masterful giving her his protection. God knows, Gerrard had never been able to feel strong and masterful where Glynis was concerned. No wonder he'd gone to the other extreme. He'd had three years of being made to feel completely weak and foolish. And he hadn't helped either. He felt a momentary contrition. It didn't last long.

He thought back to the afternoon. Glynis's phone call, her hysteria, her demand to be taken home. Her pride had been hurt, understandably. She'd hardly spoken a word on the journey down. He'd even felt sorry for her and pity was something he'd never expected to feel for Glynis.

His head jerked and he reached for a cigarette to keep himself awake. It no longer felt as if he were lying next to a corpse. Her body heat was returning, slowly but certainly. He used the candle to light his cigarette and held it above her. There were faint scars on her face, barely discernible, one high up on her forehead running into her scalp. That one looked as if it had been a bad one. He smoothed her fringe back into place, covering it up. She'd had long hair when he'd seen her before, looping back into a prim bun. It was short now, smooth and glossy with a copper sheen.

She stirred, snuggling into him like a child. He smiled grimly. She'd hate herself if she woke now. He could remember the disdainful scorn in her eyes that first time he'd seen her in the office. He'd been amused and then annoyed and he'd made some disparaging remark to his father and been slammed down with a ferocity that had surprised him so much he'd remarked there was no fool like an old fool. He'd nearly said goodbye to his five hundred then.

He wondered if his father knew about her and Gerrard. Probably not. What was she doing down here though? And with that gun? He'd have to find out before she did some damage. Tomorrow . . .

He woke with a start. The candles were guttering low. He remembered the cigarette he'd been smoking and saw it had gone out on the floor leaving a deep burn mark. Fool. That could have been serious.

He felt the girl's pulse and forehead and she suddenly opened her eyes. He stiffened, holding his breath, but her lids drooped again and she half sighed and turned over.

More relieved than he cared to admit he slid out of the bed and carefully drew the blankets around her again.

The gun. It didn't take him long to find it. He checked it over automatically and then again with disbelief, smelling at the barrel to make sure. It hadn't been fired. She must have been telling the truth.

But a gun had been fired. He'd heard it, felt it whistling past his ear, and there was the splintered headboard with the spent bullet no doubt embedded in the plaster behind. Did she have two guns then? He wouldn't have put it past her. A thorough search turned up nothing more ominous as a weapon other than a rusted sheath knife that he thought he recognized as one of his own from his boyhood days. He put the gun back under the mattress thoughtfully. If someone had been in she'd taken it very calmly. Why hadn't she had hysterics? Or at least tried to convince him that she wasn't a nervous neurotic? She must have known that was what he was thinking. Why hadn't she cared? Because she doesn't give a damn what you might think about anything he answered himself wryly. Well, Jason, as soon as she wakes up you're going to ask a hell of a lot of questions to find out what this is all about. And she's going to answer them—whether she thinks you're the biggest jerk under the sun or not.

5

ABBY woke slowly and reluctantly. She'd been dreaming. A pleasant dream for a change. She couldn't quite remember what it was about but there had been a feeling of comfort and security. She didn't want to open her eyes and face reality. And then she remembered. She wasn't in the hospital. She was in the cottage—and she wasn't alone.

Her mind wandered over the events of the night, skipping over the bits she didn't want to remember. Jason Wainwright kissing her, thinking strange things about her, looking at her with that odd expression compounded of compassion and something else, regret perhaps. No . . . wait a minute. She sat up in bed abruptly. She'd dreamed that last bit. She must have done. He'd been here, in bed with her, holding her in his arms.

She looked around her cautiously. She was in the bed by the window. There was no sign of Jason, no sign of anything to say he'd been there. Had she dreamed that too?

She put a hand to her head. She couldn't have dreamed it all. It wasn't possible. She got out of bed and went to the bathroom. There were dark shadows under her eyes, and her lips . . . No. She hadn't dreamed that then. No amount of dreaming could produce that puffy bruising.

She washed and dressed and went downstairs. Jason was in the kitchen, laying strips of bacon in the frying pan.

"Good morning," he said cheerfully. "It's a beautiful day."

She looked out of the window and granted that it was.

"Lay the table, will you?"

She looked at the amount of stuff he was putting in the frying pan. "Don't do any of that for me. I only want coffee."

"Everyone should have a good breakfast. You're on holiday, aren't you? Then start the day right." He went on slicing tomatoes.

She shrugged. She wasn't going to argue. She just wouldn't eat the stuff. She found a cloth and set the table, for one, and then opened the door and strolled as far as the bridge. The sun was bright but there was a sharp wind blowing. She turned to go back and something in the stream caught her eye, a sodden bundle of fur, orangy fur, caught up between two boulders. She went down on the bank and looked closer. Marmaduke was dead, and the water tumbled past the limp dead flesh, joyous and uncaring. She felt sick.

Stumbling she went back into the cottage, remembering the way it had leapt after the man in the night.

The smell of the frying bacon hit her stomach like a physical blow. She retched but there was nothing to bring up. Jason looked round quickly, his eyes narrowing. She held on to her stomach, fighting for control and was tempted to tell him that it wasn't morning sickness. Instead she said flatly, "Your bed warmer's in the stream. Dead."

Quick concern shadowed his eyes. She sat down abruptly and put her head between her knees. The bacon frizzled and burnt. She couldn't bring herself to go near it and then Jason was touching her shoulder. "Are you all right?"

"Oh, perfectly. This is my favourite position."

"Here ... drink this." He gave her something, she didn't know what, something fizzy and bitter. She swallowed it down and looked at him. "He was killed wasn't he? I mean he couldn't have just fallen in. Cats don't do that."

"He was strangled," Jason said curtly. He went back into the kitchen and filled the pan with water after scraping the charred fragments into the waste bin.

"I'm sorry," Abby said. It seemed a very inadequate remark to make. She added hesitantly, "He was protecting you. He must have sensed you were in danger. The way he leapt at the man ... He frightened him out of his wits. That shot at you wasn't aimed. He wasn't ready to fire."

"It damn near got me for all that. Supposing you tell me exactly what happened last night."

"There isn't much more to tell. I heard him coming and got ready for him but the cat . . . well, it took me by surprise too. I've never fired a gun, you see. I have to wait until it's just impossible to miss. There was no sense in firing just for the sake of it. That way he'd be warned for next time."

"And that wouldn't do!"

She flushed slightly, her sympathy dying an instant death. "You think I'm off my head, don't you? Do you also think I strangled the cat too?"

"No."

"Well, that's something I suppose," she said, disconcerted at his tone. "What *do* you think then?"

"I think you'd better tell me what you're doing with that gun and why someone should try to kill you."

"But it wasn't me he was after. I

thought I'd made that plain. Who knew you were here last night?"

"Hold on . . . You are the one who was expecting company. You were ready for trouble."

"But not that kind. Not a man."

"Oh? A woman then? Glynis perhaps?"

She blinked, and then remembered. "That again," she said disdainfully. "Really! The avenging wife! Even if it were true do you imagine I'd be expecting Glynis to come storming down here to do me an injury?"

"It's quite within character for her."

"Maybe so . . . but I wouldn't feel I had to have a gun to protect myself."

"So why do you have it?" he interjected swiftly.

She didn't speak for a few minutes. Did he really have no idea? Or was he so obsessed with Glynis that he couldn't see beyond the end of his nose?

"Don't you know what happened to me?" she said slowly.

"Haven't I made that obvious?"

"Don't you read the papers? Didn't the

name Abigail Burton ring a bell almost a year ago? My parents were murdered. I was left for dead. Yesterday was my first day out of hospital."

He didn't remember. It had touched no chords. Until yesterday he'd completely forgotten the name Abigail Burton. It had taken Glynis to remind him. Now he didn't think he'd ever forget.

She stared at him, at the narrowed eyes, and said scornfully, "Of course I suppose it's possible to conduct a red hot affair from the confines of a hospital bed but you will have to admit it's rather unlikely."

"Stranger things have happened." They both turned at the cool voice. Glynis was at the doorway, her dark hair immaculately coiffeured, a superb white trouser suit sheathing her figure in a severely tailored line. "Are you trying to deny Gerrard is in love with you?"

"There's no need to deny it," Abby said shortly. "It's too absurd to even consider."

"Gerrard doesn't consider it absurd.

He told me he was in love with you. There's no need for you to deny it—see, your very words. No need at all. Unless of course, now you've seen Jason, you think you might be on to better things. What did you do, Jason? Try her out? She looks as if she's had a very rough night."

"You have a nasty mind, Glynis," Jason said mildly. "Do you want some coffee?"

"Love some." She sat down gracefully, her eyes going over Abby inch by inch. She had never failed to make it obvious she thought Abby less than the dirt under her feet and today was no exception. She was gracious in the nastiest way possible. "You've certainly changed, Abigail. I would never have recognized you. You should buy yourself some decent clothes though. With all that money you've had from Gerrard you can afford it."

"What money?" Abby demanded in astonishment.

"She plays the innocent very well, doesn't she, Jason? What money indeed!

Gerrard's paid well over fifteen hundred pounds into her account these last few months."

"I don't believe you," Abby said flatly.

"Of course not. You deny it all." She smiled and looked knowingly at Jason.

"Your coffee," he said and handed it to her without a flicker of expression.

A look of annoyance crossed her face at his lack of response.

"I tell you I know nothing about it," Abby insisted desperately.

"We won't argue about it." The smile returned. She crossed her legs and settled back, stirring her coffee. "Don't be afraid I'll make a scene. I was upset of course when Gerrard sprung it on me yesterday but I've had time to think about it now and I can see the advantages of a divorce." A quick glance in Jason's direction left no doubt of one of the advantages. "You'll have to leave here though. I can't have you on my own doorstep."

"A pity about that. Because I'm not leaving," Abby said in a hard voice.

"You are, my dear. I'm telling you to go."

Abby took a deep breath. "I might have jumped for you in the office, Mrs. Wainwright—I considered it part of my job to be pleasant to Gerrard's wife—but we're not in the office now and if you're not careful I'll tell you where you can go too, and I'll be very explicit as to the precise location."

"Toast and coffee. Come and sit at the table." Jason had a hand under her elbow and she found herself sitting at the table with the wind taken out of her sails before she quite realized what was happening.

"I said I didn't want anything to eat," she protested.

"You need it. Eat." He picked up the knife and placed it in her hand, pushing the butter and marmalade towards her.

"But I'm not hungry."

He didn't say anything. He merely stood over her until she picked a slice of toast from the rack and began to butter it, then he sat down opposite her.

"You can go when you've finished your

breakfast," Glynis said. "Jason can run you into Fishguard and you can catch a train from there."

"Sorry. Count me out," Jason said cheerfully.

"Jason!" If the table had sprung up and hit her she couldn't have been more surprised. "You can't want her around."

"Why not?"

"But . . ." For once she was at a loss. Abby munched her toast stolidly and Glynis took another good look at her, a hard one. "You did get up to something last night then. Is that what it is? Why . . ."

"Glynis . . ." Jason interrupted in a very pleasant voice, soothing, almost syrupy. "She's here at the invitation of the old man. She's a favourite of his. Just think for a moment. What will his reaction be if we turf her out? You can risk it if you like but I'm not prepared to have anything to do with it."

It was almost possible to see the computer banks click into action, the pound signs rattling. Glynis relaxed, instantly mollified. That made sense. She laughed. "Trust you, Jason. I might have known you'd have some good reason. But he won't be very happy at the idea of a cosy twosome either. He's old fashioned that way. I think I'd better move in to preserve the proprieties."

"As you like." He shrugged as if it didn't matter one way or the other.

"I'll have another coffee," Glynis decided, "and then you can come and collect my things."

As if he were a lackey, ready to jump at her slightest wish, Abby thought in disgust. How could he allow it? But he merely said laconically, "I've a job to do first. I'll follow you later."

"What kind of a job?"

He refilled her cup. "A burial."

"What?" Her cup rattled in the saucer.

Abby raised her head curiously. There had been a note of horror and fear in Glynis's voice. Natural enough at such a statement? Jason seemed to be measuring his reply. "We had an uninvited guest last night."

"And you killed him?" Glynis breathed.

"No, I didn't kill him," Jason said woodenly. "He killed Marmaduke."

"Oh!" She closed her eyes for a moment. "Oh Jason! How you scared me! I had a vision of you in prison for the rest of your life. What happened? Did you get a good look at him?"

"I didn't see him at all. Marmaduke scared him off."

"Marmaduke! I don't know why you insist on calling him by that ridiculous name. What did you do? Did he take anything? There's far too much of this sort of thing going on. People aren't safe in their beds and the police don't seem to be able to do a thing to stop it. You flash your money around too much, you know. Someone must have thought they were on to a good thing. They must have seen the car and known you were down."

"Maybe."

"Are you going to the police?"

"What could they do? You're quite

right in saying there wouldn't be much point."

"Yes. True. It would only be a waste of time. He'd have worn gloves of course. They don't make mistakes like that nowadays. Not with all the crime plays on television. Everyone knows about fingerprints."

Jason nodded.

"Burglars don't usually carry guns," Abby interjected tartly. What on earth was the matter with Jason? And what was Glynis so nervous for? Talking ten to the dozen. "And they don't—"

"Drink your coffee." Something flashed from Jason's eyes. A warning? She stared at him but he was looking at Glynis again. "He won't be back. The best thing we can do is to forget all about it."

"You must be—" Abby subsided again. It was a definite warning this time. She picked up her coffee cup, staring at the white linen cloth. How gallant! He didn't want Glynis to be worried of course. Not a word of the shot that went whistling past his ear.

"What were you going to say?" Glynis demanded sharply. "And how do you know he had a gun? Did *you* see him?"

"It was dark, Glynis. No one could have seen a thing," Jason said smoothly. "And we know he had a gun because it went off. The cat probably frightened him out of his wits. I don't think he intended to fire it. Don't worry. There was no harm done."

"Don't worry!" Glynis uttered a short mirthless laugh. "You're not telling me everything, are you? You're keeping something back. And you expect me not to worry?"

"I'm not keeping back a thing," he lied with utter conviction. "There's no need to be apprehensive. You'll be just as safe here as you are at the farm."

"Oh . . ." Her lips curved in a gratified smile. "You think I might be frightened. You think I'll change my mind about coming." She stood up and patted his cheek, smiling at him as if he'd presented her with a bouquet of flowers. "Have no doubts on that score. I'm coming. But you . . ." She wheeled on Abby. "Aren't you afraid? After all that happened to you too?"

Abby glanced at Jason. Was she allowed to speak for herself this time? Apparently so. He didn't make a move to check her. "I can take care of myself."

"Can you?" Glynis smiled her disbelief. "You didn't do very well before, did you? Tell me, did they rape you as well? I wondered at the time but the papers didn't say. They were all too full of your fight for life."

"A pity, wasn't it? You and a few thousand others left to pine of curiosity. A violated virgin is so much more interesting than a couple of murders." She shook her head in wonder. "It's astonishing in what small grooves some people's minds run."

"There's no need to be insulting," Glynis said coldly.

"There wasn't," Abby agreed. "But I'm well past the stage of being embarrassed by ghoulish questions. You call the tune and I'll match you every time."

Glynis took a deep breath. "It's such a shame," she told Jason. "She was a reasonably nice girl before that sad experience. One must make allowances, however. I'll see you later, darling." She made an unhurried exit, leaving the evocative perfume of Madame Rochas in the air.

Abby began clearing the table, slamming the plates together viciously.

"I'll do that," Jason said. "You sit down."

She flared up. The last straw to break the camel's back. "I'm not an invalid and the sad *experience* has at least made me grow up and stand up for myself. And what was that charade in aid of? Were you really so worried she might not stay? I'm sorry if I've spoiled your plans for a loving weekend together."

"Liar," he said equably. "There's nothing would please you more."

"You brought her down, didn't you?"

"That doesn't mean I had an illicit weekend in mind."

"But Gerrard isn't going to like it."

"Why should he care if he's in love with you?"

"Will you get it into your head that's as likely as the Pope renouncing God. She's made that up."

"And the fifteen hundred pounds too? Glynis doesn't make up things like that."

"Ring Gerrard. You ask him. You'll probably find she's left a note saying she's gone off with you. Of course you know it was only your lack of money that made her choose Gerrard in the first place and it must have been very galling when you started splashing it around as if you'd won a fortune. You rubbed it in, Jason, didn't you? Security is all very well but there's no excitement with Gerrard and your fleeting visits couldn't have done anything but make you seem more desirable. Are you still in love with her?"

His brows came down forbiddingly. A year ago she'd have quailed. Now she smiled at him. "I never could understand why you made such a fool of yourself. It isn't as if you were inexperienced, like Gerrard. All those girls! Well . . ." She eyed him speculatively. "Aren't you going to answer?"

"It would seem Glynis isn't the only one to ask questions which are better unspoken. Why do you want to know?"

"Because a man in love can never see straight. Maybe it escaped your notice but Glynis was very upset at the thought that you might have killed our visitor last night. She was also very relieved when you said you weren't going to the police. And all that rot about you flashing your money around, seeing the car, no use looking for fingerprints. He had a key."

"I hadn't forgotten."

"Hadn't you?" She eyed him thoughtfully. "And why were you at such pains to keep me out of it?"

"I would have thought you could have worked that out easily enough. You seem to have a good imagination."

"It fails me now. The only explanation I can think of doesn't fit the facts."

"And what are the facts? Glynis wants me? Or she wants me dead? You can't have it both ways."

"I suppose I can't," Abby agreed reluctantly. Jason dead would be no use to Glynis. She must have been wrong in her interpretation of her nervousness.

"Of course," Jason said, getting out a cigarette. "She might want you dead. In fact, I'd say there was no doubt about that at all. Which makes it very convincing to me that there's something in this tale about Gerrard being in love with you. She couldn't bear anyone to beat her at her own game." He regarded Abby's darkening face with a faint smile. "You're sure it was a man last night?"

"Yes."

"Why?"

"The bulk of him, the shoes, the gloves. They fitted," she snapped, adding scornfully, "Glynis has small feet. They'd have been flapping about in those shoes like an ant lost in an elephant's footprint. Besides, can you see Glynis creeping about with a gun in her hand? She'd get someone else to do her dirty work."

"Exactly." He nodded as if he'd been

the one to make the point. "Did she know you were down here?"

"Well . . . I suppose your father might have mentioned it," Abby admitted but adding at once. "However, she has no reason to want me dead. No, don't dare say it," she warned.

Jason said mildly, "I was only going to say she could have been telling the truth about yesterday. Gerrard could have told her he was in love with you. He might have been trying to make her jealous and yours was the first name he thought of."

"Believe me! My name would be the last in Gerrard's mind. He doesn't like me. Your father is too fond of me for his liking."

"Then that's why he wouldn't have minded sending a little trouble your way. No, perhaps not," he added with regret. "That's a little too imaginative for Gerrard."

Abby said, "Isn't it rather silly kicking this around? All you have to do is ring him."

"Gerrard and I aren't exactly on very

good terms," Jason said. "He might tell me to go to hell. Still, I'll try." He stubbed his cigarette out. "I'll go and find a spade and then I suppose I'd better go and collect Glynis before she blows a fuse."

"She has only to lift a finger, hasn't she? You don't really think she's capable of murder. You're humouring me for some reason."

"Am I?" He smiled at her. "I'd never be surprised at anything Glynis did. You keep that pepper pot handy while I'm gone."

6

SHE didn't know what to make of him. It was difficult to equate this man with the charming youth who had beguiled the office girls, still less with the explosive fury of the man who had half killed his brother. He was watchful now, the impulsiveness contained and controlled. Impossible to guess the thoughts behind that poker-faced expression, the motives prompting the casually deceptive words that meant one thing to her and another to Glynis. How could Glynis believe he cared about his father's reaction one way or the other? He never had cared. And if in this instance he did, he would have never come right out to admit it. He would never be so crude. So did he want her to stay? Or was it just a way of stopping Glynis from making things awkward. He might like a peaceful existence. Or maybe he had even anticipated Glynis's reaction. It would be very convenient to have a chaperon who knocked herself out with sleeping pills at night.

She thrust him from her mind with an effort. What did she care? He was nothing to her. He could do as he chose.

It took only a few minutes to wash the dishes. She left the burnt frying pan in the sink and went for a walk.

Pembrokeshire, so John Wainwright had told her, was a land of wild flowers and birds and the cliff tops gave no lie to his words. Gulls swooped and dived far above her head and then floated in magnificent grace in some invisible air pocket; she walked between carpets of sea pinks and campion. There were more of the giant white daisies, sticking their heads out of every nook and cranny down the side of the cliffs.

She walked slowly, taking it all in, but all too soon the exertion pulled at her legs and it became an effort to keep going. She stopped at a stile and leaned against it. So peaceful. Not a sound of a car, not another soul in sight. There was another river valley stretching out behind her but no stone cottage nestled in the shelter of the hills. Only the hedges gave sign of human occupation of the land, hedges of hawthorn, bent and distorted by the strong sea winds. It would be bleak here in winter, bleak and desolate. Where would she be then? It was no use putting off all thoughts of the future. She had to find another job, somewhere to live. A flat perhaps.

"Penny for them," Jason said almost in her ear.

She jumped violently. There'd been no sound of his approach. Nothing to warn her. Supposing it had been someone else? Where would her day dreams have got her then? Annoyed with herself she said resentfully, "You could get yourself into trouble creeping up on people like that."

"People? Or a girl by the name of Abigail Burton? You little fool. Don't you know you're playing a dangerous game?"

"I don't know what you're talking

about," she said stiffly, turning her back on him again.

"Oh, don't you? Mrs. Lloyd happens to get a daily paper. And I saw yesterday's too. I also spoke to my father."

She shot round. "You didn't tell him about last night, did you? You didn't! It could kill him." In her agitation she grasped his arm fiercely.

He stared down at her, a curious expression in his eyes. "You really care about him, don't you?"

"Of course I do," she said impatiently, brushing that aside as completely irrelevant. "Why did you have to ring him?"

"Relax. I told him nothing that would set his blood pressure rising."

"I see. You were checking up on me. Was that it?"

He shook his head, not in contradiction but more in a chiding manner, and plucked her hand from his sleeve, holding it firmly.

"My child," he said. "I left in rather a hurry yesterday, after telling him I'd be staying for the weekend. I had to explain my plans were changed."

"Did you now?" Abby said sarcastically, snatching her hand out of his grasp. "You don't usually show such concern. He's used to your getting mysterious phone calls and flying off without a word of explanation."

"You *do* know a lot about me, don't you? It's beginning to worry me. However, now that I've been appointed to look after your interests I'll have time to reverse the situation."

"What! What do you mean?"

He said blandly, "My father asked me if I could spare a few days to go down to the cottage and look after you."

"He did—*what*?"

He smiled, enjoying her consternation. "He thinks you need a body guard. I said I'd be happy to oblige."

"Why didn't you tell him you were here already? Oh Glynis, of course. You didn't want him to know you'd brought her down."

"He'd have started worrying," Jason

said airily. "Far better to let him think I was doing him a favour. You should be grateful I agreed. He was thinking of hiring someone to do the job. You wouldn't have liked a stranger dogging your every footstep, would you?"

"He wouldn't have done that," Abby said witheringly.

"No? His mind was running on the lines of a strong and brawny nurse. He intercepted that telegram you sent to Mrs. McDonald and stood over her while she read it. Naturally, he had every one of this morning's papers then, almost as soon as they came off the presses. Your photographs don't do you justice, by the way."

Abby bit her lip. "Was he upset?"

"Upset is not the word." Jason shook his head at her but added lightly, "However, he's confident of my ability to make sure no harm comes to you. He has great faith in me. Why did you do it? And why didn't you tell me all about it last night instead of having me imagining all sorts of things."

"So you're convinced it was me he was after now?"

"There's no one with reason enough to want me dead. You now . . . there are three very frightened people who want you out of the way. You don't in all truth have a clue where to find them. Do you? It's a bluff. You're hoping they'll find you."

"Last night was nothing to do with them. And he had a key. You keep forgetting that."

"Don't treat that as significant. Those kind of people have special keys that will open any kind of door."

"Those kind of people! You don't know what you're talking about. That man had nothing to do with them."

"How do you know?"

"Oh! You think they hired him? A contract? That costs money. They wouldn't have two half-pennies to rub together and they'd come themselves—all three of them. They'd think it an easy job to knock me off."

"And you were going to prove them

wrong." He laughed derisively. "You've got to be kidding."

"I can see it's not the slightest use talking to you." She pushed past him and then turned back. "Did you phone Gerrard too?"

"There was no reply. That £1,500 by the way, is your salary."

Her lips parted and then tightened ominously.

He ignored the warning signs. "It's quite normal practice. Most firms see that their employees get sick pay. I'm surprised Glynis didn't think of it for it was almost the first thing that came to my mind."

"You really think she didn't know?" Abby demanded sardonically. "You really think she doesn't know the difference between the firm's account and Gerrard's own personal account? And how did you manage to slip that question in to your father? Didn't he think it rather peculiar that you should be enquiring about the state of my finances?"

"Certainly not. He'd know I wouldn't

want to be landed with your expenses." He grinned at her. "He told me to tell you about it. He didn't like mentioning it himself. Seemed to think you'd object. Can't think why. They can well afford it and it will be a while before you are able to work again."

"I can't take it. I'm not going back to work there."

"Do you think he doesn't know that? He wouldn't care if you never went back to work at all."

"You had quite a conversation, didn't you? What else did you ask him?"

"And you make out *I'm* suspicious! Come on. It's time we had some lunch."

"Where's Glynis?"

"I left her at the cottage. She can fend for herself. We're going to the pub and you're going to have the biggest steak they have on the menu. My father says I have to see you eat properly too. Apparently it's been a cause for concern. Are you afraid of getting fat again?"

"No."

"Don't sound as if you'd like to bite

my head off. You won't find it all edible, I assure you. While the steak will be absolutely superb."

"Very funny."

"I'm glad you think so. I have to humour you too."

"Don't tell me that's another instruction from your father! I won't believe that one."

"No. That one was from Glynis. I expect that will surprise you."

"Not when I stop to think. It was almost possible to see her calculations when you mentioned your father this morning. Does she imagine he'll cut her out of his will if she's rude to me?"

"You have a very nasty mind," he said severely. "She's prepared to make allowances for you so you must do the same. I cannot live in an atmosphere of discord."

"I feel sorry for you."

"Does that mean you're going to be awkward? It's totally unnecessary. Glynis assures me that she won't say one word out of place. In fact, the subject of Gerrard is strictly banned. She'll go back after the Bank Holiday and sort it all out."

"Why doesn't she go back now?"

"And leave me with you?" His eyes laughed at her. "I don't think she'd agree to that and to tell you the truth I'd sooner have her around."

"I see," Abby snapped.

"I don't think you do but never mind." He gave her a little push. "On your way."

She set off at a fast pace but all too soon the band in her chest tightened and her breath began to gush noisily.

"What's the hurry?" Jason demanded behind her. "We're not trying to break any track records."

"You needn't try to be considerate as well," Abby said bitterly. "I'm sure it doesn't come naturally. I'm pooped and I don't mind admitting it."

"Then relax and slow down. I'm not panting at your heels. A leisurely speed suits me fine."

"Which bed are you sleeping in tonight?" She swung round and caught his expression, guilt almost, and then his eyes were hooded and he said, "I suppose I'd better occupy the front room and leave the two singles for you girls."

She regarded him narrowly. "Where did you sleep last night?"

"What a question!" He laughed. "As a matter of fact I didn't get much sleep at all once that shot had gone past my ears. Anyway, why do you ask?"

"Because that second bed didn't look as if it had been disturbed and the bed in the front room was just as I left it."

"And are you suspecting I shared yours?"

She met his bland gaze and it was hers that fell. It must have been a dream. Stupid of her to bring it up. That look of guilt was for something else. For what was on his mind. Just as she suspected. She said, "I don't take sleeping pills every night. And I wouldn't advise anyone to go straying in the dark. You might warn Glynis."

"You mean I should tell her you're likely to take a pot shot at any surreptitious movements?" He was quite serious but she had a feeling that he was laughing at her again. "I think we should keep it quiet that you're a very dangerous character. We'll just pretend everything is as it should be. My sudden interest in you is due to an overwhelming attraction. I'll act the part, don't worry."

"And not explain?"

"Why should I explain?"

"I would have thought that obvious. Glynis looks on you as her personal property."

"Does she now? Then she's in for a rude awakening, isn't she? Have you got your breath back yet?"

It was no use. He wasn't giving anything away. She started walking again.

The door of the cottage was closed and there was no sign of Glynis through the window. She hesitated. "Mrs. Lloyd made a casserole. We could have that for lunch."

"Glynis can have it."

"Well, hadn't we better tell her we're going out."

"No."

That was blunt enough. She shrugged. If he wanted to store up trouble for himself, it was his business. Only let the heavens fall in on his head, not hers. She wasn't going to bear the brunt of Glynis's displeasure because he didn't want to face up to her. Glynis was too much of a bitch when she was roused.

Her mother wasn't much better. She came out of the farm house when Jason went for his car, parked in the yard. "Where's Glynis?" she demanded. "Her clothes have gone and she's not left a note or anything."

"Sorry," Jason said. "Never thought of it. You weren't around when we came to collect them. She's staying at the cottage. She thought it better with my being down and Abigail on her own. The talk," he added helpfully as Mrs. Lloyd stared at him with a frozen blankness.

"Talk!" She came into life as if a switch had been turned. Eyes flashing, a heated flush reddening her cheeks. "I'm not having my Glynis staying there. Not with her. She'll bring disaster down on her. I told her, I warned her. And now see what's happened. You fool," she swung round on Abby. "You've got one chance. One chance. This man is your life. Take him away from here and you'll be free."

"Free of what?" Abby said but Mrs. Lloyd wasn't listening to her. She advanced on Jason and said in a low voice, "It's time you followed your head. Never mind what your heart says. Get out of here and as fast as your car can take you. Otherwise . . ." The fire died out of her. She looked suddenly old and beaten and in her eyes was a great sadness. She turned away from them and walked quickly to the back of the farm.

"I can never make her out," Jason remarked morosely.

"I think she's a witch," Abby said and waited for a laugh of ridicule. But Jason didn't laugh. He said, "I often used to think that. She always had an uncanny knack of knowing what was in my mind."

"And what's on your mind now?"

"Food," he said after a slight pause.

"I see." Abby eyed him speculatively.

"I suppose that's easy enough to follow. Would that come under the heading of heart or head though?"

"And will you take me, Abigail?"

"Don't be ridiculous," she said shortly.

"I don't know that it's such a bad idea. We could go away somewhere—and I'll make sure the destination isn't published."

She swept him a disdainful look and got into the car.

"I'm serious," he said, following her. "And remember she said one chance, no more."

"To be free," Abby reminded him. "And she didn't say what that meant. She's good at that. You should have heard her yesterday. Death was reaching out to touch me and all sorts of rot. All she wants is to get me out of the way. That's what Glynis wants too, isn't it? It makes me wonder if there's some buried treasure in the cottage somewhere and they're frightened I'll start digging. Well, I'm not moving. Not for anyone and—" She paused and said slowly, "But there was a death. Did you tell her about the cat?"

"No."

"She couldn't have foreseen that. She couldn't. It's coincidence."

Jason glanced at her but said nothing, his hand on the ignition switch.

"Oh, she's mad," Abby went on crossly. "The best thing we can do is to forget her completely."

"Folks around here are a little afraid of her," Jason observed reflectively. "She has a gift of 'seeing things'. We could go to London, Abigail. It wouldn't take long. And from there we could go anywhere."

"Don't talk such utter rubbish. I'm not going anywhere with you."

"All right then." He started the car and backed into the lane without attempting to argue.

Abby glanced at his face. He hadn't meant it of course. Take her away? When Glynis was there at hand? Well, he might have taken her somewhere and a convenient phone call would necessitate some urgent business which meant his instant departure. She wasn't such a fool. There she would be, stuck in some inaccessible spot, when he'd be flying back to Glynis. Oh no. He wasn't going to do that to her. She had to keep her guard up. Remember what he was really like.

But as he stopped outside the pub she felt an absurd disappointment. He should have driven her off, overriding any protests. That was the kind of man he was. Why couldn't he be that way with her?

7

HE led her straight inside to the dining-room and left her at a table telling her he'd be back in a moment.

She guessed he was trying to phone Gerrard again but when ten minutes had elapsed she began to get restive. People were staring. She became acutely conscious of her tangled hair and dishevelled appearance. When Jason had said a pub she'd taken him at his word. But this was an hotel and the people were dressed accordingly. When the waitress arrived to take the order she found out where the ladies room was situated and made tracks for it. A comb and a wash helped somewhat, but she decided to get some make-up after lunch. With Glynis around she'd need help to boost her morale.

Jason had still not returned to the

dining-room. She glanced in the bar and then caught sight of him in the receptionist's little cubbyhole. He wasn't on the phone. He was talking to the girl there, a striking looking blonde and from the way she was looking up at him, he was talking to good effect.

She backed away quickly before he saw her and bumped into a man coming out of the residents' lounge.

He smiled and apologized and went on up the stairs leaving Abby with the tang of after-shave in her nostrils and a big question mark in her mind. That had been Howard Denning. The man who was going into partnership with Gerrard. Now what in the world was he doing here?

Scarcely giving herself time for thought she ran up the stairs and was just in time to see which room he went into. No. 6. She wouldn't forget.

She went back to the dining-room thoughtfully. Jason was still conspicuous by his absence and the melon was on the table.

She'd half eaten hers when at last he approached. He didn't apologize. Somehow she hadn't thought he would.

"Any luck?" she enquired sweetly.

"He's still not there."

"I meant with the blonde."

He raised an eyebrow. "All seeing as well as all knowing. You are a very dangerous person to have around."

"Guess who else I saw—Howard Denning. He's staying here."

"And who is Howard Denning?" he enquired placidly, not at all moved by her discovery.

"He's only going into partnership with your brother. Do you think Gerrard is on his way here too? Then we'll all be one big happy family."

"Did he see you?"

"We practically collided but he didn't recognize me if that's what you mean. He didn't come to the office very often in my time and anyway I was only a part of the fixtures and fittings. To some people typists aren't human."

"Some typists aren't," Jason asserted

and continued smoothly before she could retaliate, "Is he married?"

"Yes." She eyed him darkly. "Why?"

"Idle curiosity."

"Really?" She gave him a derisive smile. "Wondering if he's one of Glynis's conquests? I wonder if she knows he's down here. In fact, I wonder if he's down here because of Glynis."

"I suggest you stop wondering and forget all about him—and don't mention that you've seen him either."

"And why not? You don't imagine she would be embarrassed, do you? She'd love it. Two of you at it."

"At what?" he said ominously.

"Why! Chasing her around," she replied innocently. "What else could I mean?"

"I think you've said quite enough," he said flatly. "None of it is any business of yours and I'd be obliged if you'd keep out of it."

"Consider me put in my place," she murmured and finished her melon without saying another word. But if Jason chose to ignore Denning's presence it didn't mean she had to follow suit. Let him think what he liked. She still believed the target last night had been him.

Engrossed in her thoughts she finished the steak down to the last stray morsel and then had some apple pie afterwards.

Jason became quite human again. "Good girl," he said. She realized what she'd done and could have kicked herself. "If you imagine that's a great achievement on your part let me tell you that the congratulations should go to the chef. Anyone would go off their food after a surfeit of hospital fare. I'm not faddy or fussy. And now if you'll excuse me I have a phone call to make. I'll try not to keep you waiting as long as you did me."

"Who are you phoning?"

"Oh? Does it matter?"

"It certainly does—if you're planning on getting yourself into the newspapers again."

"I wasn't as it happened. But it's an idea." And then as he looked as if he was going to come with her, she said, "I'm only phoning your father. I promised to call every day."

"That's all right then." But he did go with her and asked the blonde to get the number for her.

"You needn't wait," she said accepting the receiver.

"You mean you don't want me to hear what you say?" He smiled at her. "Very well. I'll be in the bar."

John Wainwright's first words were to ask if Jason had arrived. He sounded immensely relieved when she told him they'd just had lunch together. "He'll look after you," he said in approval, "and make sure you don't do anything silly. Do what he says, Abigail. Promise me."

"It depends on what he tells me to do," she said sourly. "You seem to forget that he can do some very silly things too. Who's to put the curb on him?"

He laughed. "You'll never do that with Jason. But he's got a good head on his shoulders for all his faults. He wouldn't do anything stupid where you're concerned. Not when . . ." He coughed.

"But never mind that. He's never broken a promise to me and I don't think he'll start now. What did he say when you first met?"

"I don't think I can remember the exact words," she said carefully.

"But he was surprised, wasn't he?" He chuckled as if enjoying a huge joke.

"Oh, he was surprised all right," Abby said dryly. "Considerably."

"He wouldn't believe me when I told him how you'd changed. He thought I was being funny."

"I'll bet he did."

"What's the matter, Abigail? You sound most peculiar."

"What exactly did you tell him? You must have dangled some other carrot in front of him—besides telling him what a knockout I've become."

"Now Abigail . . . I don't like to hear such cynicism. He was delighted at the thought of—" Even he realized that his choice of words was scarcely credible to anyone who knew as much about Jason as Abby. He added earnestly, "But I didn't have to persuade him. I assure you that he agreed without any argument." She let it go. He was feeling too good. Whatever anxiety he'd suffered at her rash actions he was confident that with Jason around no harm would come to her. So let him think it.

When she'd finished talking to him she paid for the call and said casually, "I believe you have a Mr. Denning here. When did he arrive?"

The girl knew without looking it up. "Yesterday."

"Is he alone?"

The girl looked at her curiously and asked a question of her own. "You *are* with Mr. Wainwright, aren't you?"

She knew very well she was. Hadn't he asked her to get the number for her? But Abby said, "That's right."

"Would you tell him that Owen is in the public bar now. He wanted to have a word with him."

"Yes, of course. About Mr. Denning . . ."

"I'm sorry. I can't gossip about the

guests." The girl flashed a smile at her and bent her head to the accounts again.

Thwarted and a little puzzled Abby passed the message on to Jason who was cradling a large brandy in his hands.

He put it down immediately. "Wait here for me. Oh, do you want a drink?"

"I don't drink."

"Oh no. I forgot." His eyes laughed at her. "And you don't smoke either. What a good girl you are. I won't be long."

She gave him a minute and then followed him. The public bar was hazy with smoke, a couple of men were playing darts, another pair had a cribbage board on the table in front of them and they were eating huge chunks of cheese spread on French bread with enough pickles to make their presence smelt a mile away. She didn't see Jason at first and then spotted him with an old man with a face as wrinkled as one of last year's apples. The man was looking at Jason as if he was speaking in a foreign tongue and then his face cleared and he broke into a spatter of talk, his arms waving in the air.

Abby went forward quietly.

". . . easy," the man was saying. "The fire exit at the end of the corridor and away at the back. No one would be any the wiser. What's the trouble? Are you—" He faltered as he spied Abby and Jason turned swiftly.

"I'm going shopping", she said. "You can catch me up when you've finished."

"All right." His face was blank. She turned, conscious that he was waiting until she'd gone before he resumed the conversation. What on earth had they been talking about? And who exactly was Owen?

She went out of the hotel and bought some make-up absently. A torch too. One like Jason's, and then some rope-soled shoes. A tiny bikini caught her eyes. She got that too and then found an absolutely glorious shop down by the cathedral. When she came out of there she'd nearly cleared out her wallet but she had a jerkin and skirt in welsh tweed and a blouse with immensely full sleeves, together with a Japanese wind charm made of slivers of intricately shaped glass which she'd fallen in love with at first sight.

Her arms loaded with her purchases she headed for one of the wooden forms in the walled circle at the bottom of the street and waited for Jason to find her. A spattering of rain changed her mind. She took one look at the darkening sky and picking up her packages set off hurriedly for the shelter of the hotel, bumping into Jason half-way up the street. He relieved her of her burden and steered her into a café. "It's only a shower," he said.

"Some shower." She stared gloomily out of the plate glass window. People were scurrying for shelter, the street of leisurely, brightly-clothed holiday makers emptying fast.

One man alone walked stolidly, oblivious or uncaring of the rain beating down on his bare head. Howard Denning.

Abby glanced at Jason but his eyes were on the waitress who was going around in circles, completely flustered by the sudden influx of customers.

"I've just remembered something," she said. "I won't be long."

She was on her feet and away before he could say a word and then she was running back to the hotel.

A man was behind the desk. She took a chance and said boldly, "No. 6." He handed her the key without a word and she went up the stairs, restraining herself from breaking into a run or looking behind her with an effort. So many guests, constantly coming and going, and if he was only relieving the blonde while she had her lunch she should be safe. No sense in taking chances however, and she hadn't much time. She locked the door behind her and looked around. A single room. A small weekend case. Empty, except for a couple of handkerchiefs. One shirt, shaving articles and a plastic wash bag, pyjamas under the pillow, a top coat in the wardrobe. The drawers were empty. He didn't intend to make a long stay then.

Pockets. She gingerly felt in the top coat and came out with a dirty handkerchief. In the other pocket her fingers closed on something smooth and cool. She was pulling it out when she heard the door handle rattle.

She froze, shrinking inside the wardrobe. It could be the maid. She'd have a pass key. But it was more likely to be Denning. He'd have asked for his key, and been told it wasn't there. What would he think now? He was hardly likely to assume there was someone searching his room. No, much more likely that he would decide they'd not looked properly for the key, or it had been put on the wrong hook.

She listened hard. There was no further noise. She regarded her find. A chamois leather driving glove. She put her hand in the pocket again and brought out its mate. New, but there were furrows in the soft leather on the backs of them. She stuffed them in her jacket pocket and went to the door. No sound outside. She opened it cautiously afraid that he might be lying in wait for her but the corridor was empty. She put the key in the lock outside and shut the door. Let him think what he liked so long as he didn't see her. It would do no harm to rattle him a little. She sped the other way along the corridor. There should be another way out. A fire exit.

There it was, clearly marked. There was a bolt on it. She drew it back. An iron staircase led to the yard at the back of the hotel. Anyone could get out and back in again and no one would be any the wiser.

A fire exit, the end of the corridor, no one any the wiser. The very words Owen had used. No wonder they had sprung to her mind so easily. And the blonde— shutting up like a clam when she'd started to question her and yet talking freely enough to Jason, putting him on to Owen too.

She ran down the steps and back to the café. Jason said irritably. "Where've you been? Your coffee's gone cold."

"It doesn't matter." She didn't really want it. So much exertion and excitement after that heavy meal had made her feel sick. She tasted it and pulled a face. "I think I've got indigestion."

"You shouldn't rush about," Jason said without sympathy. "You didn't answer my question. Where have you been?"

She eyed him guilelessly. "I got some gloves. I must cash a cheque too. I've spent nearly all my money."

"It's Saturday afternoon," he reminded her. "Do you want to buy anything else now?"

"No," she said doubtfully. "I don't think so."

"I wouldn't think so either," he said, picking up the packages meaningly. "We'll put these in the car and then I'll show you the cathedral."

The sun had come out again by the time they reached the end of the street and they joined in the stream of holiday makers making their way towards the cathedral. It lay in a hollow and coming on it unexpectedly Abby caught her breath at the loveliness of its situation, rolling green turf, the ruins of some great building behind, the dignified simplicity of the cathedral itself.

"Two pilgrimages here equalled one to Rome," Jason told her. "To the English at that time it was the end of the world." He gave her a guided tour, pointing out the various things he thought would interest her and afterwards they went on to the ruins of the Bishop's Palace. It was quiet here, with only the odd people around. Very different to the crowds in the cathedral. "I spent hours here when I was a kid," Jason said. "Climbing around and around those spiral steps, trying to get as high as I could and then lying with the sun on my face imagining how it used to be. It must have a magnificent place in all its glory. Come on up."

He led the way, ducking his head to enter a dark slit. Abby followed with some misgivings but once started had to go on. Around and around, he'd said and he'd not exaggerated. She got claustrophobia and she was breathing hard when they came out on to a narrow parapet.

There were no rails. She looked down and vertigo promptly took the place of the claustrophobia. She sat down, gripping hard on to the stone and watched Jason scale an open flight of steps to a square look out point.

"Come on," he called.

She gritted her teeth. Admit a weakness to him? Never! "In a moment," she said brightly and waited until he was out of sight before she moved, using her feet and hands as the means of locomotion with her bottom never more than two inches from safety.

Backwards down the steps. Definitely. Much safer. She could go on using her hands.

She never felt what hit her. One moment the light was telling her she was almost back to the first floor level, the next it was blocked out and then she was lying flat on her back and Jason was bending over her asking her what had happened.

She stared at him blankly. What a

stupid question! How was she expected to know?

"Did you fall? Abigail! Answer me. Lord!" He ran his hands over her limbs. "Is anything broken? Does it hurt? Abigail! Say something, for the love of Mike!"

"My head hurts," she said obligingly and tried to sit up. It did hurt, and far more in a vertical position. She groaned and he slid his arm around her. "Let's see. You must have banged it against something. There's a lump the size of an egg."

"Don't touch it," she screamed thinly, too late. A wave of sickness passed over her. She closed her eyes.

"The skin's not broken," he assured her.

She didn't care. She wanted her pills and she'd left her handbag in the car, thinking she wouldn't need it. "Get me some aspirin or something," she said desperately. "No, don't move me," she cried as he attempted to pick her up.

"But—All right. Here boy! Stay with this lady, will you, until I get back?"

She opened her eyes and through a blurred mist saw a duplicate version of a small boy standing near by. She closed her eyes again. It could be twins but more likely she was seeing double. How could she have hit something? In that position? Her bottom would have made contact first.

She clapped her hand to her pocket. The gloves were still there. It hadn't been Denning then. Or had it? He might have seen her and followed her to retrieve his property but he could have been disturbed. It depended on how quickly Jason had arrived on the scene.

"Did she take something?" the boy said.

"What?" She painfully brought him into focus. Yes, one only. A snub nose, freckles, bright eyes, dirty jeans and a violently striped tee-shirt.

"She was bending over you. She ran away when the man started to come down."

"What was that?" Jason said quietly. He had a plastic cup full of water and a packet of anadins in his hand.

While his attention was on the boy Abby took the lot. She was taking no chances of them not working. Unconsciousness was better than the feeling that she had three heads, all of them outsize and filled with pounding hammers.

The boy was repeating himself with relish to Jason who demanded, "Are you sure it was a woman?"

"It looked like it," the boy said, but added with engaging frankness, "But I find it a little hard to tell sometimes."

"What was she wearing?"

"Well..." He frowned. "Jeans I think, some kind of trousers anyway, and a shirt and great big sunglasses. That kind of white blonde hair like Jimmy Saville's."

Despite her condition Abby didn't fail to hear the breath expelled from Jason. A sigh of relief? She glanced up quickly; too quickly. Pain lanced through her head and brought a return of the double vision.

She saw two of Jason as he fished in his pocket and tossed some money to the boy. "You've been a great help. Thanks."

"Cor! Ta. D'you want me to be a witness for you?"

"No thanks. Though I don't know. Hang on. Give me your name and address just in case."

Full of self importance the boy imparted both his home address and that of the place where he was staying that week. He ran off clutching his money ecstatically.

"He'll probably make himself as sick as a dog now on chocolate and ice cream," Abby commented, trying to get to her feet.

It was an effort and she wouldn't have made it but for Jason's helping hand. "Can you walk?" he said.

"I guess so," she said grimly. She wasn't going to have him carrying her anyway.

"We must have been followed here," Jason said grimly.

"Yes." Abby was having second

thoughts. Had she been the target last night after all? Certainly no one could have mistaken her for Jason this afternoon.

"That settles it," he went on grimly. "We're getting out of here."

"I didn't think you were a coward, Jason. Is it your habit to run away from trouble?"

"A tactical retreat isn't running away."

"In my book it is. Have you ever seen Glynis in a blonde wig?"

His face closed up and became remote and withdrawn. She knew about tactics too. And as a diversionary one Glynis was completely successful. Jason didn't mention going away again. He couldn't get back to the cottage quick enough.

8

SHE slowed him down. She couldn't help it. Every step pounded at her head. When they did get back Glynis was stretched out on the couch, reading a glossy woman's magazine, the fire crackling in the hearth. She looked as if she'd not stirred all afternoon.

"Where have you been?" she demanded.

"Showing Abigail the village," Jason said. "Been out?"

"I was waiting for you. You didn't say you'd be so long." She leaned over and got a cigarette from a box on the low coffee table by the couch. She was wearing a long red housecoat with deep revers fastened by a broad belt alone. She didn't appear to have anything on beneath it. "You look a little peaky, Abigail," she said. "Has he worn you out?"

"I have a headache," Abby said

shortly. "I think I'll go and lie down for a little while."

"I'll bring your stuff up." Jason followed her.

Glynis had taken over the wardrobe and piled the top of the chest of drawers with her toilet articles. A black chiffon night dress was strewn across the bed.

Jason dropped Abby's packages on her bed and went through the wardrobe and then the drawers. "Satisfied?" he asked her harshly.

"She's not stupid," Abby said. "You surely didn't expect to find jeans or a blonde wig here? No, of course you didn't. I'm the one you think is stupid."

"I think you're . . ." He didn't finish. Swallowing the words with a visible effort he slammed out of the room.

She picked up the nightdress disparagingly. Black chiffon! Trust Glynis. Had she really not moved out of the cottage?

It could have been one of those three. They could have seen her in the village and followed them, waiting for a suitable opportunity. It had been deserted enough for them in those ruins, especially when Jason left her alone. It could be her dislike of Glynis was making her as prejudiced one way as Jason was the other.

She cleared the bed and lay down on it, closing her eyes. It was dark when she opened them again. The pain in her head had completely gone and she felt better than she'd done for a long time.

A candle was burning and someone had covered her with a blanket. She got up and went to the bathroom. The lamps were lit in the room below. She could see Glynis, still on the couch, but there was no sign of Jason.

She ran the water and decided it was hot enough for a bath. It was nearly ten o'clock when she went downstairs again. She'd almost changed into her new outfit until she thought of glancing at the time. A waste of time getting up really but she'd not sleep now for hours.

"So you've decided to join me," Glynis said. "I was beginning to think you'd retired until morning." She had a transistor playing softly and a chunky glass in her hand. Scotch, if the bottle on the coffee table was anything to go by. "Do you feel better?"

"Much, thank you." She couldn't help noticing the ash tray. It was almost overflowing. Earlier on there'd been a couple of stubbed cigarettes, no more. Now if Glynis had been in all afternoon . . . Oh, stop it, stop it, she told herself. "Where's Jason?"

"He went for a drink."

Never let me out of his sight, she thought in bitter quotes, and knowing how I feel about Glynis he's left me alone with her. In fact he'd probably done it deliberately. What did he expect? That she'd make another attack on her here? Then it would be proof? "Wasn't there enough for him here?" she said aloud, eyeing the scotch.

"You know men . . . well, maybe you don't! They have a preference for draught beer in the convivial atmosphere of the saloon bar. He wanted to take me with him but I thought you might be alarmed if you woke up and found yourself alone."

I'll bet, Abby thought. At least he wouldn't have done that. Left her alone in the cottage. Or would he? She didn't know him well enough to be able to say that with much conviction.

"Would you like a drink?" Glynis asked. "Or maybe something to eat."

"I'll get something."

"No, you sit down. Jason told me what happened this afternoon." She rose gracefully, the long folds of the housecoat swirling around her legs. "What would you like? Something light at this time of the night? An omelette perhaps?"

"That would be fine. Thank you."

She sat down and listened idly to Glynis bustling about in the kitchen. She'd not bothered to draw the curtains properly. There was a good gap of about a foot. After a while she began to feel someone was staring at her from the darkness outside. I'm getting a persecution complex she thought and went to the window. Nothing moved outside. She was letting her imagination run away with her again. Nevertheless she drew the curtains closely together.

"There's no need to be nervous," Glynis said. "Jason has fixed a bolt on the door."

So he had. A good strong one. "Has he been out long?"

"About half an hour."

So he'd waited until he heard her get up. How considerate!

"Here you are." Glynis brought the omelette out on a tray.

She would have to be a good cook too, Abby thought sourly. The omelette was perfect, filled with cheese and garnished with tomatoes.

"Now how about some coffee?"

There had to be a catch. Glynis had to be up to something. The coffee was sweet and milky. Too sweet to hide something that might be bitter? Her sleeping pills. Had Glynis been up to the bedroom and with the pretext of leaving the candle rifled her handbag? She couldn't very well check on them now. Besides she didn't know how many she had, or should have had.

Glynis was watching her from her chair; cat-like eyes, intent and watchful.

Abby took another sip. "It's very hot," she said and reached out to place it on the low table just as a knock sounded on the door. It was very easy to fake a start and drop the cup.

"It's only Jason," Glynis said and went to open the door. "You frightened poor Abigail," she said. "She's spilt her coffee all over the floor. No, don't bother about it," she said as Abigail went on her knees. I'll make some more. You'll have some too, Jason?"

"Why not." He went over to Abby and helped her to her feet. "I'll wipe that up. How do you feel?"

"Fine."

There was not the slightest whiff of beer on his breath.

He got a cloth and mopped up the spilt coffee and Glynis brought more out, telling Abby to be careful and not to drop this one.

She didn't think she could. Not again. She watched Jason drink his without a murmur or a grimace and said abruptly, "I thought there was someone watching us from outside. Did you see anyone hanging around?"

"No, but I'll take a look." So that got rid of Jason. But Glynis wasn't going to go anywhere. She sat tight, still watching her.

Abby raised the cup and swallowed half the coffee and then got to her feet quickly. "I'll wash up."

She went into the kitchen and shut the door over Glynis's protest, not a very convincing one, and turned the taps full on and made herself a drink of salt and water, forcing it down. A few mouthfuls were enough. She gagged and gasped and the coffee did a quick round about turn and ended up in the sink.

She washed and wiped up, feeling guilty but much better.

Jason started yawning about twenty minutes later. She followed suit and said earnestly, "I can't understand it. I've only been awake about an hour and I'm ready for bed again."

"It's only to be expected," Glynis said. "You look tired too, Jason."

"Yes. I'm for bed." He rose to his feet.

"I think I might have a bath," Glynis said. "I'll try not to disturb you."

Abby followed Jason upstairs. Should she warn him? He'd only turn that remote face on her and not believe a word. Anyway, it was too late. If the coffee had been drugged it would be well into his system by now.

She got into bed with the gun under the pillow and the torch down at her side.

It seemed an age before Glynis came into the bedroom. Abby lay on her stomach, her face hidden in the pillow. Now she'd know for certain. She tensed herself for a hand on her shoulder and a hearty shake but Glynis didn't come near her. Instead there was an almost imperceptible rustle. The chiffon nightdress? Yes. She turned her head and opened her eyes the merest slit. But Glynis didn't get into bed. She picked up the candle and left the room.

Abby strained her ears. No creak of the stairs. Had she gone into the front room? She felt a most peculiar wrenching of her stomach. How silly of her. She should be glad she'd sleep safely in her bed. But Jason faking his tiredness, pretending . . . No, he hadn't pretended. She should have known. She *had* known.

She turned on her back. In a year a youth could change into a man, his shoulders could broaden, habits could change. One of them might have even turned respectable. He'd be all the keener to bury his past.

Denning's presence could probably be explained. So could the state of his gloves. Glynis's attitude *had* been explained. What was she lying here worrying for?

Noise. There was no sound from the front room. Surely they'd talk a little. And that bed had creaked, hadn't it?

She got up quietly. Glynis had closed the door. But surely she'd still hear something. She opened it cautiously.

Glynis hadn't gone in the front room after all. She was downstairs again. Abby stood there watching her. She'd turned the lamps out. There was only the light from one candle placed on the table beside the bottle of scotch. She was standing in the middle of the room, her head cocked as though she were listening. Had she heard her get up? But she wasn't looking upwards. She moved towards the door and drew back the bolt. As she opened the door, the draught blew out the candle. Abby strained her eyes, telling herself not to jump to conclusions again. Glynis could merely have been looking out. But she'd been listening for something, or someone. Not that that meant anything either. Still . . . She went for the gun and the torch, hurriedly stuffing her clothes under the blankets to make it look as if a figure lay huddled up there. If she found a knife tear there in the morning that would be proof enough for Jason, or would it?

His door was half open. She edged around into the room. Glynis hadn't relit the candle and the stairs were creaking again. It could be Glynis but why hadn't she heard her go down them?

With every nerve on edge, every sense straining to work to its utmost she was ready for anything but an attack from behind.

A hand over her mouth stifled the startled cry that tore from her throat but her fingers tightened involuntarily around the gun and it went off with a bang that sounded like a clap of thunder in the still silence of the cottage.

She felt it wrenched from her hand and then she was bodily lifted and thrown into the bed. "Don't say a word," Jason whispered savagely into her ear.

She couldn't if she'd wanted to. She was stunned and breathless and slightly deafened by the shot.

There wasn't a sound from outside the room. It was as if everyone was holding their breath and then there was a rush of footsteps. Glynis called out. She sounded frightened. "Jason! Jason! Are you all right?"

"Sorry, Glynis." He went out of the room closing the door behind him, but though his voice was muffled Abby heard him plainly enough. "We had an accident in the dark."

She was out of the bed like a pea from a pea shooter, opening the door a crack to listen better. Glynis was downstairs, lighting the candle with shaking fingers. "I was just on my way to bed. Silly! I dropped the candle. It—it sounded like a shot."

"Only a chair going over," Jason said calmly. "You've stayed up very late."

"I was thinking, wondering—" Her voice sharpened, she blinked. "Did you say *we*?"

"Don't act so surprised," he said, his voice lazy with amusement. "She's a nice girl, a little impulsive perhaps, but then aren't we all sometimes."

"Jason! I don't believe it. How—"

He yawned and patted her shoulder. "It's too late to talk. I'm sorry we frightened you. Is the door bolted?" He checked it and started back up the stairs. "See you in the morning, Glynis."

"What on earth do you think you're doing?" Abby hissed at him furiously as he came in at the door.

"Shut up," he said coldly, "and get back into bed." He switched on the torch and found where the bullet had gone. Smack into the floor by the skirting board.

He dug it out with a penknife and hacked at the hole to disguise how it had been made and then jammed a chair under the door handle and switching off the torch got into bed beside her.

"I demand to know what you're playing at," Abby whispered, temper nearly making her whisper a shriek. "I mean, it's not a habit of mine to go sneaking off into someone's bed. If you really want Glynis to believe you we'll have to be a little more friendly at other times too. You've not exactly been showing much sign of this overwhelming attraction for me."

"What did you come into this room for?"

"Well, it wasn't to make love to you. I was coming to warn you."

"Why?"

"Glynis let someone in."

"How do you know?"

"Oh, very well. I *thought* she had let someone in. My goodness! If she only knew how you protect her and then you spoil your chances by playing out a little charade like that. Or perhaps you were trying to arouse the devils of jealousy in her? Will you explain it all in the morning, after a suitably emotional scene of course. A nice girl but so impulsive? You *couldn't* turn her away. You're far too kind-hearted."

"Will you get to sleep."

"I won't. I've never felt more wide awake. Why don't you want Glynis to know I have a gun?"

"You don't. I've got it."

"You will return it," she said at once.

"No."

"But I'm in danger. And a fine bodyguard you make. You go off and leave me alone with Glynis when you are very well aware of how I feel about her."

"I was outside watching every move you made, until you drew the curtains on me."

"Oh!" That was very deflating. She recovered valiantly. "I did notice the absence of a beery smell from you and wondered what you'd been up to, and I did feel someone watching, didn't I? I told you so. Did you see her make the coffee?"

"She can't have put anything in it. You're all right, aren't you?"

"I made sure of it," Abby said smugly. "I brought it up with salt and water. Still, I suppose you're right. I was expecting to find it impossible to wake you."

"As to that . . ." Jason said reluctantly. "I got rid of it too."

"How?"

"I put my finger down my throat."

"Glory be! You do think she's up to something then!"

"No, I don't. I'm just not taking any

chances. And if you'd not come barging in my room tonight we might have known one way or the other. I could wring your neck."

She edged away from him. He sounded as if he meant it.

"Oh, look . . ." He raised himself up on his elbow. "Will you please trust me and not go off on a tangent of your own? I won't let anyone hurt you—and I mean anyone. Act normally with Glynis and pretend you've fallen for me."

"Oh, that will be nice for me. Doting sheep's eyes and all that rot. Why, for God's sake?"

"Because," he said patiently, "then you wouldn't want me out of your sight and it will also make tonight more convincing. Do you imagine I want Glynis to know that I suspect her of trying to kill you? And apart from anything else, if by some crazy chance you are right, it's better that she doesn't know you're toting a gun. Not that I think you are right. Not for one moment."

guard you make. You go off and leave me alone with Glynis when you are very well aware of how I feel about her."

"I was outside watching every move you made, until you drew the curtains on me."

"Oh!" That was very deflating. She recovered valiantly. "I did notice the absence of a beery smell from you and wondered what you'd been up to, and I did feel someone watching, didn't I? I told you so. Did you see her make the coffee?"

"She can't have put anything in it. You're all right, aren't you?"

"I made sure of it," Abby said smugly. "I brought it up with salt and water. Still, I suppose you're right. I was expecting to find it impossible to wake you."

"As to that . . ." Jason said reluctantly. "I got rid of it too."

"How?"

"I put my finger down my throat."

"Glory be! You do think she's up to something then!"

"No, I don't. I'm just not taking any

chances. And if you'd not come barging in my room tonight we might have known one way or the other. I could wring your neck."

She edged away from him. He sounded as if he meant it.

"Oh, look . . ." He raised himself up on his elbow. "Will you please trust me and not go off on a tangent of your own? I won't let anyone hurt you—and I mean anyone. Act normally with Glynis and pretend you've fallen for me."

"Oh, that will be nice for me. Doting sheep's eyes and all that rot. Why, for God's sake?"

"Because," he said patiently, "then you wouldn't want me out of your sight and it will also make tonight more convincing. Do you imagine I want Glynis to know that I suspect her of trying to kill you? And apart from anything else, if by some crazy chance you are right, it's better that she doesn't know you're toting a gun. Not that I think you are right. Not for one moment."

The poor sap. He was fighting to believe in Glynis. Every inch of the way.

"Why did you pretend you didn't know Denning?"

"I don't."

"You were asking the blonde about him and then you were trying to discover if he could have got out without anyone seeing him."

"So you were listening. I thought so."

"I merely heard enough to put two and two together," she said modestly. "What put you on to him then?"

"Glynis phoned someone there," he said unwillingly.

"What did she say?"

"Nothing out of the ordinary at all," he said coldly. And he turned over with such finality she didn't dare open her mouth again.

9

JASON had gone when she woke up. Glynis too, was not in her bed when Abby went to get dressed. She felt an extreme reluctance to go down and meet the eyes of either of them.

She needn't have worried. They were at the table and whatever words they might have had, an amicable agreement seemed to have been reached. They both greeted her cheerfully and Glynis asked her what she would like to eat.

Not to be outdone in politeness she insisted that she finished her own breakfast and made some scrambled eggs on toast for herself.

No reference was made to the night before. Glynis asked if she'd like to go for a swim after breakfast. "It looks like being a hot day," she said.

Sticking to her role, Abby dutifully

turned to Jason and asked him if he was going.

"I might as well." No smile. A somewhat ungracious acceptance of her. So that was how he was going to play it. She was doing all the chasing. How perfectly in character! That overwhelming attraction must have stuck in his throat. He couldn't bring himself to pretend that in front of Glynis.

She wasn't looking so good this morning. In fact she didn't look as if she'd slept very well. Pique? Or conscience?

Abby tucked into her scrambled eggs with relish. She decided she was going to enjoy the day. Even the fact that she was left behind in the shallow water while Jason and Glynis took off for the horizon didn't worry her. She splashed about happily. Glynis looked good in a white costume but her bikini was just as fetching and she wasn't making a mess of her hair either.

She spread her towel on the beach and waited for them there. She should have got some sun cream. Sun glasses too. The glare hurt her eyes as she lay on her back. She sat up again.

"You didn't stay in long." Glynis strode out of the water, her skin glistening, a flush on her cheeks. The swim had rejuvenated her. She no longer looked tired. She rubbed her hair in the towel and then began to brush it over her head, her face hidden. "Too cold for you?"

"I'm not a great swimmer." And that was the understatement of the year. She could just barely swim.

"You're wise not to go out of your depth then."

Abby glanced at her sharply, suspecting a double meaning and Glynis swung her hair back. She was smiling. "Yes. You don't know what you've taken on. What are you hoping to get out of it? I'd have sworn you were the type who holds out for the ring on her finger."

"Then I wouldn't be bothering with a married man, would I?" Abby said very softly.

"What do you mean?" Glynis said blankly.

She had forgotten about Gerrard. Forgotten all about him. Or rather what he was supposed to have said. Lies were easy to forget.

"I'm referring to your fairy tale of Gerrard being in love with me. You knew that money was my salary, didn't you?"

"Oh! So that's what you're going to say? Good thinking. It sounds almost feasible." She flung her towel on the sand and stretched out on it.

"Jason believes it."

Glynis leaned up on her elbows and coldly surveyed Abby. "Jason's mine," she said. "He always has been and he always will be. You might think you've won him from me but it will take more than a romp between the sheets to do that. He has these little affairs. I don't mind. But how will you feel when you realize he's only using you?"

"There comes a time when all good things come to an end," Abby said lightly. "And that applies to you as well,

Glynis. You've had your day. I know what Jason wants and I can give it to him. This time isn't like the others."

And that was true enough. If Jason heard her now the wringing of her neck would almost without doubt become a certainty.

"For one thing I know all about you, for another, this is what his father wants." She smiled, full of her own power and the vividness of her imagination. "He'll marry me, and believe me, you won't get within a foot of him again without my being right there at his side."

"You are very sure of yourself," Glynis purred but some of the confidence had left her eyes. "However, you've a long way to go yet."

"You mean he doesn't love me? True . . . but as soon as he finds out his father has changed his will I don't think he will hesitate."

That was the way to do it. The way Jason had done it. Glynis would believe anything if she saw a monetary benefit in it for someone.

"Changed his will?" she said in a blank sort of disbelief that yet believed.

"He's very fond of me and of course I've no one now." Abby lay on her folded arms. "He wants to make certain that I'll never lack for anything in my life. You think Jason is down here because of you, don't you? But his father asked him to come to look after me. That's the real reason."

"I don't believe you," Glynis said flatly.

"Ask him." She turned over indifferently.

"Jason . . ." He was just coming out of the water. Glynis sprang to her feet and went to meet him. "Did your father ask you to come down here to look after Abigail?"

Jason hesitated only briefly. Abby smiled to herself. He'd see nothing wrong in confirming that. "What of it?"

"Then he did!" Glynis faced him stormily. "Don't you see what she's done. He'll make sure you marry her now. You know what he's like."

"Don't be ridiculous."

"But Jason—" She turned from him almost blindly and snatching up her towel ran back towards the cottage.

Abby looked back at Jason. He was frowning, staring after her flying figure. "What have you been saying to her?" he demanded.

"I was merely carrying out your instructions. She's convinced now that I'm hell bent on getting you one way or the other."

"That wouldn't upset her."

"That's what I thought you had in mind. Only you see I also convinced her that I'd succeed."

"I don't believe you. She'd laugh at you."

"Dear me. Are you so unattainable? Actually she did laugh—at first. And then I told her your father had changed his will and somehow she got the impression that if you married me you'd end up with all his money. That was when she stopped laughing."

"You're cleverer than I thought."

"I'd thank you but I don't think you mean that as a compliment somehow." She smiled at him. "If it bothers you why don't you tell her that I was lying, mop up her tears and convince her that wild horses wouldn't drag you to the altar with me? You don't care about money—even if she does."

"You might have thought you were lying," Jason said with his eyes as flat and cold as packed ice, "but you were close to the truth."

She stiffened. "What are you saying?"

"My father *has* changed his will. He told me yesterday. You'll never have to worry about money." His gaze bore hard down. "The prospect of wealth doesn't seem to delight you. Are you afraid of the strings attached?"

"You don't mean—" She swallowed hard. "He wouldn't."

"Why not? It sprang to your mind easily enough. Would you marry me if it meant being rich?"

She got to her feet, picked up her towel and bag and faced him. "You think to show me I can be just as mercenary as Glynis, don't you? You think I'd do it even if I denied it right now. Well, let me tell you something, Jason Wainwright. I'd marry you if it meant losing the money, every penny of it, so stuff that in your pipe and smoke it."

She stalked off, her back rigid with resentment. If that didn't put him in his place, nothing would. And then full realization of what she'd said hit home. She must have been mad! What had she said? She missed her footing on one of the stones by the stream and flung a startled glance behind her. He was standing stock still as if she'd shocked him into complete immobility.

As well she might. She scrambled up to the cottage, her cheeks flaming fiercely. Supposing he believed her. Supposing ... oh, it was too awful for words.

She tore up to the bedroom and dived into her slacks and sweater. Glynis was in the bathroom.

She rushed into the front room and looked out of the window. Jason was still on the beach but he was making tracks for the cottage. She nearly broke her neck jumping down the stairs and set off at a run along the cliff path.

He saw her and shouted but she kept on going. He wouldn't follow her. He'd have to change first. She ran until she could run no farther and then as soon as she got her breath back she ran again.

She passed the lane, down into Caerfai Bay up again between the ferns and gorse and then she steadied to a walk. There were other people on the path now. She saw the sign for St. Non's Chapel and went to take a look at it. It was incredibly tiny, built in 1934 by the owner of the nearby house because his wife had turned Catholic and the nearest church was fifteen miles away. The stone for it was brought from the ruins of various churches, central heating had been installed and services had been held there but in spite of the special waterproofing and the two and a half foot thickness of the walls, in the severe weather the rain from the sea went through as if it were cellophane. It didn't seem possible on that bright and sunny day.

She paused by the wishing well and tossed a coin into the water and then took the lane into the village, walking slowly now. There were tall stately foxgloves in the ditches, their bright purple catching the eye and completely overshadowing the pink campion and the mass of Queen Anne's Lace.

She sat on a form looking down on to the cathedral and watched the people treading lightly down and toiling, not so lightly, back up again.

"Why did you run away?" A shadow loomed over her; the seat plunged, then steadied. Jason sat down beside her.

"Run away? Why should I do that?" She kept her eyes resolutely fixed on some children chasing a ball. She might have known he would find her. She shouldn't have run. She should have kept her dignity.

"That was what I was asking you. I've been looking all over the place for you."

"Don't tell me you were worried?"

"Would that be so unnatural?"

"I think so."

He was silent. Presently he said, "It wasn't true what I said. There aren't any strings."

"No, I didn't think so." She felt suddenly very tired.

"Let's go and eat," he said.

She got up without a word and walked by his side up to the hotel.

"We'll have a drink first." He shepherded her into the bar, hesitating in his stride for a moment.

Glynis was at one of the tables with Denning.

"Look what I've found," she said brightly. "Jason, this is Howard Denning, he's joining the firm. Howard —my brother-in-law. And you and Abigail know each other I think."

"Oh yes." He stood up to shake hands. "You worked in the office, didn't you?"

"Yes."

"What are you having to drink?"

"A bitter lemon, please." She sat down

after a glance at Jason. She had to remember her role after all.

He got beer for himself and Jason, scotch for Glynis.

"What are you doing in these parts?" Jason said casually, taking a long pull at his beer.

"Following my profession," Denning said. "You know how it is."

"No, actually I don't. Have you a client down here?"

Denning glanced at Glynis. "Oh, I don't mind them knowing," she said impatiently. "Howard's doing my divorce for me. He wants to talk to you, Abigail."

"She's nothing to say," Jason said at once.

Glynis sighed. "Lift up your visor, Sir Galahad. I think you'll agree that it will be better all round if we have a very quiet, quick, uncontested divorce. Once Gerrard discovers his precious Abigail is having a fling with you he'll do all he can to drag you down. And he'll be able to do it too, won't he? Your name will be spread over all the Sunday papers."

"That will worry me."

"Oh I know you don't care what anyone thinks of you but if Gerrard is smearing my name I'm not going to sit back and take it, Jason. I'll retaliate, with Abigail." She nodded, her lips pursed a little. "That's different, isn't it? Your father won't like that at all. In fact, I'd say it's almost a certainty that he'll make another new will, wouldn't you?"

Jason took his time getting out a cigarette, not answering.

"What is it you want me to do?" Abby asked politely.

"Nothing very much at all. A short statement. And I think perhaps you'd better not be seen with Jason until it's over. Gerrard might find out about it."

Abby broke into an involuntary laugh, startling both Glynis and Denning. Jason's expression didn't change at all.

"You mean I'd better go away?" Abby enquired. "And at once of course. No, my dear . . ." She mocked Glynis's patronizing tone perfectly. "It won't work. Retaliate? With me? Mr. Wainwright knows me better than that. He won't believe any of the lies you concoct."

"I don't need to concoct a thing," Glynis said coldly. "And if you have no regard for the state of his health, maybe Jason has. I understand any worry or upset could be fatal." She kept her gaze fixed on Abby. Never mind Jason. She had picked on the one spot where Abby was vulnerable and she knew it.

"I'm driving back after lunch," Denning said casually. "I could give you a lift."

"It's really in your best interests," Glynis added. "After all, it does seem as if you're in some danger down here. It will be better for you to be out of it."

"I'll let my father know you're coming," Jason said. "He'll be glad you've changed your mind."

That last felt like a hard jab in her midriff. Right where she had least expected it. The look she turned on him was that of a wounded doe. He ignored it and said briskly, "That's settled then. Now how about some lunch?"

He didn't care. He wanted her out of the way as much as the others did.

She took no part in the conversation flowing so brightly and easily over the lunch table. Glynis, her objective achieved, was bubbling over with good humour striking sparks off both the men.

Picking her way through food that tasted like sawdust and ashes Abby tried to dismiss the suspicion that the three of them had been working together with the one aim in mind. It was only Jason who knew how much the thought of upsetting his father meant to her. There'd been that curious look in his eyes when he realized it. Had he seen it then as a potential weapon? Had he primed Glynis? The set up in the bar—where he had taken her. Oh yes. She'd thought he wouldn't be crude but he was a shade more devious than she had imagined. All that rot about trusting him. It was only what she should have expected. And she was a fool to feel as if she'd been betrayed. He'd not promised her anything. He was sending her to his father—who no doubt would be delighted with him for succeeding where everyone else had failed.

Only where did Denning fit in? Why had Glynis asked him to come down? Really. That excuse of the divorce was laughable.

She pushed the food around on her plate, eyeing him covertly. He was the same age as Gerrard, they'd been at university together. They were friends. And yet Denning had come down here as soon as Glynis called. He must have done. Another man in love with her? And driven mad by the thought that she could be in love with Jason he had attempted to kill him? And that was the most ridiculous notion she'd come up with so far. Denning didn't look as if he'd ever had a consuming passion for anyone or anything. He was a big, thick-set man whose heavy jowls and fleshy body betrayed a love of food and drink and a sad lack of exercise. In a few years' time his good looks would probably disappear in the mounds of fat that already threatened but now his tailor hid the bulk of it and his profile was only marred by the weak set of his mouth. He talked well. He alone of the three seemed to recognize that there was a fourth person present and he addressed some of his remarks to her even though he didn't seem to expect a reply.

As far as Glynis or Jason were concerned she could have gone up in a puff of wind and neither would have noticed. She wished a little wistfully that she had long black hair and was beautiful and then despised herself for the thought. She didn't care how Jason felt. She didn't. Let them do what they liked. She wouldn't even ask if Glynis was still staying on at the cottage. She agreed apathetically to Jason collecting her things and at three o'clock was sitting in Denning's car ready to leave.

"Take care," Jason said, leaning over to say goodbye. "I'll see you soon."

"Don't strain yourself, please."

"It's better this way. Don't—"

"I understand." She cut him short. "I

must have been a great worry to you. Goodbye, Jason."

"Do you like him so much?" Denning asked as he turned into the road.

"I don't know what on earth you mean," she said coldly. "I hardly know him."

"That wasn't the impression I had from Glynis."

"Impressions can be very misleading. For instance I received a strong impression that you had come down here for quite a different reason from the one you gave Jason."

"Oh?" He shot her a quick, startled glance. "And what was that?"

"Maybe Gerrard sent you. Maybe he wanted proof that his wife and Jason were having an affair."

The relief in his eyes was too great to be missed. He blinked rapidly, gave her a weak smile and said, "Supposing you were right? I've a fine tale to tell now, haven't I? I wonder," he added reflectively, "if Jason could have thought that too. He's always been very clever.

Gerrard hasn't been able to catch him out yet."

She smiled, even though she could gladly have reached out and raked his face with her fingernails. That relief on his face though. It showed he had a guilty conscience. "You mean," she said sweetly, "that Jason took me to bed instead of Glynis because he'd found out you were around?"

"He has a sixth sense," Denning said. "It's got him out of a lot of trouble."

"And I suppose when you saw Glynis and told her what Gerrard was trying to do she decided to get in first. You did tell her, didn't you?"

"Now hold on there. You're jumping to too many conclusions. I'm not saying anything but that Jason is a very clever operator and a sweet innocent child like you is better out of his way."

"So that if someone crept in on them tonight they'd find Glynis instead of me?"

The car jerked forward under the pressure from the acceleration pedal but

Abby kept her eyes fixed on the face of the man beside her.

"Glynis won't be at the cottage tonight." he said harshly. "She's not such a fool."

"Are you sure of that?"

"Of course I'm sure."

"Why?"

She might have slapped him across the face. The effect of the abruptly spoken demand was stunning. He stuttered as he tried to sort out if there were any implications that he had missed.

"Whatever is the matter, Mr. Denning?" Abby said mockingly. "Your nerves seem to be in a shocking state, I only meant that if *you're* out of the way and *I'm* out of the way, they've got nothing to worry about, have they? So why should Glynis move out?"

He ran his tongue over his lips. "You're forgetting her mother. She would never allow anything like that."

"Yes, of course." She clucked her tongue. "How silly of me to forget. So anyone creeping in would find Jason all on his own. It will be a disappointment, won't it? By the way, where is Gerrard? Couldn't you have arranged it so that he would burst in on them?"

"All this talk about creeping in and bursting in on them. It's silly," he burst out. "The mere fact that they stayed the night together would be proof."

"But not as good as a few lovely flash photographs. Have you got a camera, Mr. Denning?"

"No, I have not," he snapped. "And you've got the wrong idea completely. I didn't—"

"You didn't what?" Abby said very softly. "Go creeping in the cottage with a camera? No, of course, you didn't. You *knew* Glynis wouldn't be there, didn't you? There wouldn't have been any point. Unless you had something else in mind?"

It had been him. She was sure of it. Every vestige of blood drained from his face and a beading of sweat appeared on his upper lip. If she were to slap his gloves down in front of him now he'd probably have a heart attack, or crash the car. She could feel them in her pocket, bulging the material, but it was time to cool him down before he did either, or think to shut her mouth for good. The only trouble was she couldn't think how to do it. Well, she'd said enough that was so far off the mark he had to think her stupid. All she had to do was confirm the impression and convince him she was an absolute idiot.

She gave a little laugh. "But that's silly, isn't it? I can't picture you creeping in the dark at all. We are sort of creeping along this road though. Am I supposed to be admiring the scenery?"

"It's very beautiful," Denning said with an effort.

"It's incredible to me that there aren't hordes of cheap stalls and boarding houses along here. Such a vast stretch of beach and completely deserted. No . . . I see a couple up there." She prattled on, saying the first thing that came into her head.

Newgale was passed, then Haverfordwest. She was running out of things to say by the time they reached Carmarthen but Denning had settled down. The way she'd been talking the most suspicious of men would have come to the conclusion that she was the most inane twit of their acquaintance.

He stopped in Cardiff and took her for some tea, dallying so much that she began to wonder when they would reach Manchester. Then when he got in the car and the engine wouldn't catch she began to do some adding up. The way he'd crept along nearly all the way from St. David's, his certainty that Glynis wouldn't be at the cottage that night, getting Abby herself out of the way. They wanted Jason alone—she'd been right first time. And now they were going to try again.

She watched him lift the bonnet and start to fiddle deep inside. He had to make it look convincing; he was bound to be some time.

Stealthily she tried the glove compartment. It was locked. Well, that was a good indication that the gun was there.

She removed the keys from the ignition and opened it.

She was right. The gun was at the back, wrapped in a duster.

She unloaded it quickly and put it back, locking the compartment again and then she dropped the bullets down the grid as she got out of the car to ask Denning what was wrong. Let the rats bite their teeth on them. They weren't going to tear their way into Jason's flesh.

Denning kept up the charade for some time, telling her he couldn't understand it, he didn't know what was wrong and then he told her that the best thing to do was to spend the night in a hotel and he would get someone from a garage to take a look at it in the morning.

She accepted it from him without a blink, thoughtfully unlocking the door at the back as he got the cases. He would have to wait until she'd gone to bed. Accordingly five minutes after she had ostensibly retired she was making her way back to the car where she made herself as comfortable as possible down on the floor at the back.

She didn't have very long to wait and then had to endure an exceedingly uncomfortable journey all the way back to St. David's. He drove erratically, sometimes with his foot so hard down that she was holding on for grim death in an effort to keep herself from being flung around, other times he drove so slowly that she found her eyelids dropping and wouldn't have been at all surprised if they'd gone into reverse. Once he muttered, "It's madness. Utter madness."

When he stopped the car he remained in his seat for a long time before he sighed and unlocked the glove compartment.

She waited a few minutes and then raised her head cautiously. They were outside the village. It was just possible to make Denning out moving along the road. She opened the door and slid out, stretching luxuriously, and then heard him coming back, at a run.

She grabbed her bag and shut the door, crouching down and hoping that he wouldn't go round the wrong side of the car in mistake.

He didn't. He flung himself in the driver's seat and started the engine. She dived for the ditch and went down flat as he turned and set off back down the road as if the devil were right behind him.

10

HE'D got cold feet. She didn't blame him. Only what was she going to do now? No hotel would take her at this hour, without any luggage. She was without enough ready cash on her either. Just as well she had some excuses ready because she knew in her heart she had no intention of going anywhere but back to the cottage.

She trudged down the lane. The farm was in darkness; not even a dog barked as she passed through.

The cottage was in darkness too. She still had her key and it opened the door. No bolt on? Did Jason think there was no need because she was no longer there or had Glynis contrived that? She would have made sure Denning could get in.

She groped her way into the kitchen and found the matches. With one of the candles lit she started to climb the stairs.

She didn't see Jason. His voice came out of the darkness; very wide-awake and very angry. "What are you doing here?"

"I came back," she said simply.

"I can see that."

"Denning came back too. He had a gun. It was him the other night but this time he got frightened and he's gone back to Cardiff."

"Leaving you to break the glad news?"

"Silly. He didn't know I was still with him. I have really been extremely clever. The car had a breakdown. He did very well at pretending but of course I knew what he was up to and I hid in the back when he thought I was safely bedded down in the hotel he picked out. Why didn't you bolt the door? Did Glynis have something to do with that? I take it she's not here."

"No, she's not," Jason said grimly, "and she had nothing to do with the bolt being undrawn."

"Still standing up for her? Your loyalty does you great credit! I expect you're thinking that I'm making up all this, don't you? Well, think on it. I'm going to bed."

She was asleep within seconds and was roughly wakened early the next morning by Jason. "Glynis is coming," he said. "I want you to stay up here and keep quiet. Will you do that for me?"

"Why?"

"Because I ask you to." He gave her a shake that made her wince. "Do you understand?"

Yes, she understood. That much at least. She nodded her agreement and he left her to greet Glynis. "You're up bright and early. Anything wrong?"

Glynis sounded quite normal. It was a pity. But then how did a person sound when they expected to find a dead body and instead the person came bounding down to greet them? Disappointed, astounded or what? She'd had practice of course. Abby tried to think back to how she'd been that first morning and almost missed the next few words. Not that they were important. Jason was asking her if she'd had breakfast and she said she'd been up for hours.

"I've been thinking about you, Jason," she said. "You seem to have put up a barrier between us. Is it that girl?"

"Could be."

Abby got out of bed and went to the door. She wasn't going to miss one syllable of this.

"You're not in love with her, are you?"

"Madly and passionately," Jason said lightly. "How about some coffee then?"

Abby's lips tightened. Of course he knew she'd be glued to the door listening to every word but he didn't have to make fun of her. Glynis however didn't seem to be at all certain that it wasn't for real.

"You don't mean that," she said unsteadily.

"Don't I? You should know, better than anyone. Why did you ask me to bring you down here, Glynis?"

"Maybe it was a mistake," she said soberly. "I wasn't thinking very straight. It was falling right into Gerrard's hands, wasn't it? Maybe that was what he intended. He's been suspicious for a long time. You know that. You've been playing on his nerves with just that intention, haven't you? Why, Jason? Do you hate him so much? Or were you trying to wreck our marriage?"

"Is it such a good marriage?"

"I made a mistake. I knew it almost at once but there was nothing I could do about it. I'd have been happy enough if you'd left me alone but you didn't, did you? And now . . . what now? Gerrard will divorce me."

"On what grounds? There's nothing he can prove."

"I can provide him with proof," Glynis said slowly. "And I will unless . . ."

"Unless what?"

"Unless you convince Gerrard that there's nothing between us. You owe it to me, Jason. Be fair, admit it. And now you're going to leave me with nothing if you go off with Abigail. I could spoil that for you, one way or the other, and unless you square things with Gerrard for me I'll do it. Go and see him. Now, today. Show him that you're not down here with me and convince him that there has never been anything between us. You can lie so well, Jason. You should be able to put something over. Say you were needling him, that was all. Say whatever you like —and while you're about it you can find out for yourself why he told me he was in love with Abigail."

"That sounds like a good idea," he said slowly. "Yes, I'll go. Mind if I finish breakfast first?"

"Oh Jason." Her voice caught in her throat. She said a little unsteadily, "I wish things had been different. I wish—"

"That I'd been solvent?"

"It would have helped," she said frankly. "Money matters to me, Jason. I'm sorry, but I can't help it. You don't know what it's like to live as we did, every penny watched and accounted for. I had to be safe. I loved you. I did. But Gerrard offered me so much more and he gave me everything I wanted."

"Everything?" Jason questioned so softly Abby barely heard him.

"Everything within his power." She laughed shortly. "It wasn't his fault that I found out it wasn't enough. It was yours. Now go, Jason. Before I start crying for what might have been."

"You're not staying here?"

"I can't stand it at the farm. My mother is going around bleating about disaster falling down on my head. She's driving me round the bend. I don't know what has got into her. Send Gerrard down here. Tell him I'll be waiting for him."

"Wait at the farm, Glynis. It will look better."

"Oh, all right," she said after a moment's hesitation. "I suppose you're right."

"I'll get my gear." Jason bounded up the stairs and stuffed his few things into the airline bag. "Clear up," he shouted down. "If you want to speed me on my way," and with Glynis in the kitchen he went into the back bedroom.

"You stay here," he told Abby. "Don't move outside until I get back—and keep out of sight."

He didn't wait for an answer or any comment and presently the cottage was still and silent.

Abby went to the front bedroom and stood watching them until they were out of sight.

She couldn't fault Glynis. The honest, direct approach. It had been perfect. It even had her wondering—again—if she'd made a mistake. She certainly couldn't blame Jason for doing what she asked.

She checked that they'd locked the door behind them and made herself some breakfast.

Glynis had left her glossy magazines behind. She leafed through them. Time dragged. How long before Jason got back? It could hardly be much before nightfall.

She made some coffee and stood drinking it before the window. What would Denning do when he found she'd left the hotel? Make a frantic phone call to Glynis?

And then Glynis would be bound to see if she'd come back here. A flash of red moved on the cliff path. For a moment she thought it was some kind of thought fulfilment but it was Glynis, in the flesh, and coming fast. She froze for a paralysing second and then ran for the bedroom.

Her bag! She'd left it on the couch. She flew down the stairs again and retrieved it. That coffee cup too. No time to wash it. Upstairs she went. Where to hide? Under the bed? No. If Glynis were looking for her it would be very ignominous to have to crawl out from under there. She would wait behind the door. She felt sick as she heard the key downstairs.

But Glynis didn't attempt to start a search. She waited downstairs. There was a click of a glass, the bubbling rush of liquid. Drinking so early? Something on her mind. She paced the floor, opening the door and then shutting it again. And then Denning arrived.

He met with a cold reaction. "You goofed—again. Did that girl scare you off?"

"I didn't know she'd gone until this morning. I told you. Her bed hadn't been slept in, she'd left her case and I didn't know what on earth to tell them. Where could she have gone?"

"It doesn't matter. We needn't concern ourselves with her anymore."

"But she was suspicious. She didn't believe anything I told her. I could see it in her eyes. Supposing she guessed I was coming back here last night? Supposing she followed me?"

"Well, she wouldn't get far at that time of the night," Glynis snapped. "If she tried it, she'd be stranded somewhere. Now forget about her. I thought of something else. Jason's gone to see Gerrard."

There was a crash, the splinter of broken glass. Denning appeared to have dropped his drink. "He—he's what?"

"Don't worry," Glynis said scornfully. "In a little while I'll be phoning the police." She laughed. "With a bit of luck they'll catch him doing something very naughty indeed. If I know Jason his first reaction will be to hide the body. He won't want the police doing any investigating on him."

"You fool," Denning choked. "They can put a time to the death. They'll know he didn't do it."

"Not even when I confess that I was there. That I witnessed the whole thing? Gerrard bursting in and catching us in bed together and going berserk. Oh, I'll make it sound good. It was self defence. Jason couldn't help himself. He had to fight back. I'll be totally on his side. That will make it much more convincing. I'll say we panicked and could only think of getting away but then Jason began to talk of hiding the body and covering things up and I realized that no one would believe it was an accident then. Informing the police was the only thing I could do to stop things being much worse."

"But he'll deny it all."

"Of course. And what good will it do him? Gerrard's suspicions of Jason were well known and I have all the letters Jason has sent me. He won't have a leg to stand on."

"It sounds too easy," Denning said worriedly.

"Yes. I can't think why it didn't occur to me before. So much better than Jason committing suicide in a fit of remorse for killing his mistress's husband. That wasn't quite in character. They might have investigated further."

"Jason will guess what actually happened though."

"They'll expect wild accusations from him. He'll be fighting for his life after all. I'll stand firm however. Don't worry, Howard. I won't let you down."

"The girl! What will she think?"

"Why shouldn't she believe what everyone else will be believing?"

"She was here that night. She heard the gun go off."

"You forget those three young men who murdered her parents. She thinks she was the target that night. After all, one of them tried to kill her the next day."

"You shouldn't have done that, you know. You might have really hurt her."

"Dear, dear." Glynis couldn't have cared less. "I wanted to give her a good fright and send her packing. And I'd have hit her a lot harder if I'd known what she was going to do that night. Spoiling everything. Still," she added cheerfully, "it's turned out for the best."

"I suppose you're right. I wish she hadn't disappeared though. I don't like unexplained factors. She could be anywhere."

"So you said on the phone. It at least provided you with an excuse to return. I had to tell you what was happening. I think our story had better be that I phoned you for advice. As Gerrard's friend, and coming into the firm as well, you were the natural person to turn to. You can say you were the one who advised me to go to the police. How about that? We can't hide the fact that you came down here."

"No," Denning agreed heavily.

"Right then. It's almost twelve. He should be getting near the end of his journey. I'll go and phone now."

"I'd better come with you—in my role of family solicitor and friend."

"Don't be bitter," Glynis said lightly. "Everything will turn out just fine."

Abby forced her tensed muscles to relax as they left the cottage. Her head was whirling. Gerrard dead! It was all so clear now. Why on earth hadn't she considered that possibility? And Jason was heading right into a trap. It would close on him and he wouldn't be able to do a thing about it. He wouldn't do the natural thing and call the police. Of course he wouldn't. He'd go on shielding Glynis right to the end.

She sat down on the bed and put her head between her hands. What could she do? There was no way of getting hold of Jason and stopping him.

Hang on. She jerked to her feet. There was a way. She could talk to someone. Someone important too. Not some anonymous policeman who would answer Glynis's call.

She picked up her bag. Glynis wouldn't phone from the farm. She wouldn't want her mother to overhear something like that. If she could get her phone call in first . . . She hurried so much she almost caught up with Glynis and Denning. She dropped back, her heart thudding in her breast and didn't move forward again until they were well out of sight again. She did make sure they didn't stop at the farm however and breathed a sigh of relief when they went straight past.

Mrs. Lloyd answered the door to her and rather grudgingly agreed that she could use the phone. "It is private," Abby said. "Could you . . ." She glanced at the kitchen door meaningly and smiled. "I would be so grateful."

With John Wainwright providing the money to pay a lot of her bills she couldn't afford to be awkward. She went into the kitchen without a word.

Abby waited until she had closed the door behind her and then asked the operator to put a personal call through to Detective Inspector Foster. He'd been the man in charge of the Burton case. He came on the line almost immediately and greeted her with a snap in his voice. Of course! He wasn't pleased with her. Not after her remarks to the press.

"Do you want to know about a murder?" she enquired plunging straight in and ignoring his implication that she should have been locked up when she left hospital. "Gerrard Wainwright was killed at his home on Friday afternoon. You'll probably find his body in the bedroom. He disturbed his wife and her lover, a man called Howard Denning, and they killed him and also tried to kill his brother, Jason Wainwright, intending to pass it off as a suicide so that he would be blamed for it." She paused, met with a complete silence and went on. "You will shortly be receiving a phone call from Gerrard's wife telling you that Jason is about to hide the body. They've changed their plan and—"

"Hold on . . . hold on. Give me those names again and don't gabble this time."

She repeated herself, fretting with impatience. "You must get there right away. Before Jason arrives. She's going to say she was there with him. She's going to claim he was her lover. She's—"

"How do you know all this?" he interrupted. He was so calm, so placid, she could have screamed at him.

"I heard them talking. Her and Denning."

"Do they know you heard them?"

"No, of course not. Do you think I'd be here telling you if they did? They're killers. Don't you understand?" She nearly did scream then.

"Where are you speaking from? Give me the phone number."

She told him, gabbling again despite herself.

"I'll phone you back," he said. "Calm down. I'll do what I can."

Calm down! She replaced the receiver and stared at it unseeingly. Would he do anything? He hadn't seemed very interested. Maybe he didn't believe her. Or thought she was getting all excited about something she'd misunderstood.

It was only his manner. Stop worrying. How could she expect him to get excited over something that could be only routine to him.

She crossed the floor swiftly, suddenly beset with the suspicion that Mrs. Lloyd had been listening at the door but she was over at the sink up to her elbows in soap suds.

"Do you mind if I wait?" Abby asked. "He's phoning back."

"Please yourself." Mrs. Lloyd didn't even turn round. She wasn't interested at all. So much for her suspicions.

She sat down and closed her eyes. Foster was a good man. He'd move swiftly and set things in motion at once.

God! She'd not given him the address. She started forward but immediately relaxed. He'd probably found that out even before she'd rung off.

Now if only they got there before Jason, before he had time to put his fingerprints all over the place.

They'd find Denning's somewhere. It couldn't have been his first visit to the house, or to the bedroom, and even if Glynis had thought of fingerprints—as was more than likely. She'd thought of it at once at the cottage—they couldn't have wiped everything clean. Surely not.

It was only her word against theirs though. If they found nothing . . . If there was nothing to link Glynis to Denning in the way Jason was linked . . .

She slumped in the chair, feeling terribly weary. A fine convalescence this was turning out to be. Even worse than she'd anticipated. Her head ached, the thoughts bouncing like a hard rubber ball rebounding fiercely from one blank wall to another. What would Jason do? He had been in love with Glynis. He had almost killed Gerrard once. Too many people knew that. And was he still in love with her? The letters he'd written. Were they old ones? They couldn't be if Glynis was planning to use them.

The letters! She stiffened, the weariness forgotten.

Would Glynis have brought them down with her? Or had she left them at the house for the police to find?

She glanced at the kitchen door. It was

still firmly closed and Mrs. Lloyd had looked as if she'd be at the sink for some time. Anyway she could always say she was looking for the bathroom.

She went upstairs like an eager bloodhound on the scent and found Glynis's bedroom on the second try.

One of her cases was locked. A good sign? She tried the key of her own case in the lock but it wouldn't budge. Well, Glynis was going to find out anyway. She got out her nail scissors and dug them into the softer leather at the top of the case. Making a hole was easier than cutting. Her scissors would never be the same again, but then neither would the case. She inserted her hand in the hole she'd made, recoiling as her fingers encountered something alien and yet somehow human. She tore back the flap and made the hole bigger. It was a wig. A blonde one.

She hesitated and then left it there, going for the pouched pockets at the back of the case.

Yes. There was paper there. Letters.

Tied up in pink ribbon. God! Glynis was overdoing it there.

Why had she brought them with her? For safe-keeping? Or had she planned on leaving them in the cottage to be found with Jason's body?

She glanced through them, odd phrases leaping from the page to hit her with sickening force. No wonder Glynis had kept them. If ever a man had loved it had been Jason. And he hadn't bothered dating them, most of them didn't even have an address at the top.

Could the police tell their age from the ink? It wasn't worth the risk of keeping them. For that matter they needn't have been old ones. No, they had to be destroyed completely.

She stuffed them in her bag and went downstairs again, pausing in sudden fright as she heard Glynis's voice. "Who was she phoning?"

"Mr. Wainwright I expect. Who else?"

Abby didn't wait to hear any more but went back up the stairs quickly. She had no intention of bumping into Glynis.

Maybe Mrs. Lloyd would think that she had got tired of waiting and had left the farm house. Maybe . . . All she had to do was to get out without anyone seeing her.

She opened the first door she came to. It was a little back room piled high with lumber.

She went to the window. There was a sloping roof to an outhouse immediately below. She couldn't hope to find a better way out from this level. She opened the window and climbed out, dropping dubiously on the tiled roof. One of the tiles went clattering down to the gutter which didn't make her feel very happy.

Gritting her teeth she followed it more slowly. There was a drop of about ten feet to the ground.

She peered over. She was right over a window. That wouldn't do. She went to the corner. Drop or jump? She dropped and fell over, wrenching her ankle as she went clumsily on to the ground. But there was no outcry. She hadn't been seen. She picked herself up shakily and made for the cottage. Speed seemed essential. If

Glynis had any suspicions that was where she would head for too but despite her efforts she couldn't maintain a run.

If Jason only knew what I'm going through for him she thought grimly, and tried to put mind over matter and forget her aches and pains in imagining how he would express his gratitude. He probably wouldn't thank her. No. Even with her vivid imagination she couldn't picture that.

She reached the cottage and immediately bolted the door.

Matches! She got them from the kitchen and knelt before the hearth, feeding the letters one by one to the ever increasing flames, then when there was nothing but the charred fragments left she set to work with the poker. No one would be able to make anything out of that pounded ash. No one. But to make certain she'd get rid of even that. She went into the kitchen again and got some paper, shovelling the ash on to it. Down the loo, flush it away.

She was going up the stairs when a key

grated in the lock. She didn't bother to investigate but rushed to the bathroom and chuted the ash down the lavatory, pulling the chain forcefully. Was it Glynis?

She went to the front bedroom and looked out of the window. There was no one at the door. No sign of anyone anywhere. Had she imagined it? And then she thought of Denning the night before. He'd expected to get in some way, and if Glynis had had nothing to do with the unbolted door she'd have left a window open somewhere.

She went downstairs quickly but she was too late. Glynis had climbed in by the kitchen window and was standing at the doorway.

"So," she said grimly. "You came back."

"There's no law against it. Where's Jason?"

The taut lines on Glynis's face relaxed slightly. That was it. Pretend she had only that moment got back. She couldn't know. She couldn't have been up to her bedroom and seen her mutilated case. "You came back because of him?" she said, raising her eyebrows. "I'm sorry for you. But you couldn't say I didn't try to warn you."

"What do you mean?"

"He's not here, my dear. He's gone to the police and given himself up. He murdered Gerrard."

"Is that so?"

Glynis stared at her, her eyes narrowing. "Don't you believe me?"

"You'll try anything to keep him, won't you? Am I supposed to rush away in horror and think what a lucky escape I've had?" And that's what she should do. Get safely out of the way. What did she think she could achieve now?

"If you wait until the morning papers are out you'll find proof enough," Glynis said.

"I can wait."

"What did you leave Howard for? Without taking your case? He found it very embarrassing to explain to the hotel people."

"I'm sure he thought of something to say." She moved to a chair and froze. That pink ribbon, so meticulously tied around the letters, lay on the hearth rug.

She looked at Glynis and saw she had followed her gaze. Their eyes met.

"When did you get back?" Glynis said after a pause which seemed to last a century.

"It took a long time," Abby said carelessly. "St. David's isn't the best of places to hitch a ride to. Most people have never heard of it."

She bent down to pick up the ribbon but Glynis was quicker. She snatched at it, staring so hard at it in her palm it could have been a snake about to bite. "Where did you get this?"

"It's not mine," Abby said with perfect truth.

Glynis sniffed audibly, her nostrils flaring, and stared at the hearth. "You've been burning something."

"Is that a crime?"

"You've been at the farm. You've

stolen my letters. My mother didn't know where you'd gone to."

"It's a mistake to keep old love letters," Abby said lightly. "They're much better out of the way."

Why go on pretending? There was nothing Glynis could do to her.

It was the biggest mistake she had ever made.

Glynis picked up the poker. "Why did you do it?" she said ominously.

"Don't be silly," Abby said nervously, quailing and changing her mind about admitting a thing. "Why do you think I did it! You threatened Jason. I don't want you supplying Gerrard with ammunition like that. Maybe he doesn't mind being a spread for the Sunday papers but I do. His father wouldn't like it."

"Did you read them?"

Abby kept her eye on the poker. Glynis wasn't holding it for mere effect. Did she want her to say yes so that she could force her to testify against Jason. "Ancient history always did bore me," she said. "Why should I bother to read them?"

"I could kill you," Glynis breathed.

Abby had no doubt that she could, or at least make a try. She edged towards her bag on the table.

"I'm going to teach you a lesson you won't forget in a hurry," Glynis said. "Did you honestly think you could steal from me and get away with it? Did you think you'd be basking in Jason's gratitude right now? Only he's not here to protect you, is he? He's a long, long way away. No! Keep away from that bag." The poker came down with a crash as Abby reached out. She paled. Another inch and it would have hit her hand. And with that force there would have been more than one broken bone.

"You think I don't know what you've got in there?" Glynis said. "You think I don't know a gun shot when I hear it? A chair falling over! What were you firing at? What did you see?"

"It was an accident," Abby said.

"Why did Jason lie to me?"

"He didn't want to upset you. What

else? You know why I've got it, don't you?"

Her brow cleared. "I thought that was why he'd done it, though why he should think I'd be upset . . . It would be very easy to kill you, Abigail, and get away with it. You've given yourself far too much publicity."

Abby didn't like the look in her eye at all. She said quickly, "Don't you think the police would think it very strange if you were involved in two murders?"

Glynis stepped backwards and Abby realized she'd made another mistake. "Two murders?"

"You did say Gerrard had been murdered . . . remember?"

"No! It's not that. You know. Don't you? You know! I can see it in your eyes."

As she spoke she raised the poker again and Abby jumped up on the table and kicked out with her legs, sending Glynis staggering backwards. Taking a flying leap Abby descended on her and sent her to the floor and they rolled over and over, fighting and kicking and grappling for possession of the poker.

Glynis was fit and strong. After the initial set back at being knocked to the floor her superior strength began to show and Abby began to realize she was going to be lucky to get out on top. She put the last of her diminishing strength in an effort to free herself instead of getting the poker, balling her fist and trying to catch Glynis a knock out blow on the chin. She connected. In fact she thought she'd broken her hand.

She couldn't hold Glynis up as her body came sagging down, the poker falling from her hand and her eyes going all glassy and unfocusing. Grunting and gasping for breath Abby pulled herself out from under and unsteadily got to her feet but her knees had barely straightened out when Glynis came round and grasping her ankles hard brought her down again.

This time she had no chance. Glynis pinned her down easily, her knees jamming her arms into her body and her hands at her throat. "What is it you know? Tell me."

"You've had it, Glynis," Abby gasped. "I was upstairs this morning when you were talking to Denning."

"You little fool. Don't you know you've just signed your own death warrant."

"I called the police—right away. If you're going to try for a self defence plea you won't be helping yourself by killing me."

"You're lying. Right from the start you've done nothing but lie. You're afraid. You'll say anything to save your neck."

"Are you going to kill me to find out how wrong you are?"

"Yes," Glynis said, and she began to squeeze her fingers tightly around Abby's throat.

11

SHE opened her eyes to the darkness of a tomb. She tried to move and could not. So this was what it was. Just a black nothingness. But her throat hurt. It was hard to swallow. She couldn't be dead. Glynis must have thought it better to put her somewhere first and check whether she had been telling the truth. She forced her senses to sharpen. She was cramped up in some sort of box. Was that wood against her knees? Yes, it was wood. But it was cold at her back. Plaster or concrete. Her feet were bound together and her hands tied in front of her. She tried to get up to a sitting position bumping her head on something hard. She felt it with her cheek. Hard and round and smooth and cold. A pipe of some sort. A waste pipe? The cupboard under the sink. That was it. She felt much better deciding that. A box conjured up so many horrible things.

She edged around so that her back was against the wall and lashed out with her feet at the wooden door of the cupboard. It shivered and shook but held firm. Infuriated with her own weakness she tried again. It should have been a doddle. A flimsy cupboard door like that.

Glynis must have left the cottage. She didn't come running at the noise.

At the third try the wood splintered and gave, her feet going through it. She enlarged the hole and wriggled inelegantly through on to the kitchen floor.

She'd guessed right. It had been the cupboard under the sink and she knocked over the pans Glynis had piled neatly on the floor. Her hands and feet were tied with a stout thick cord. She'd need a sharp knife to free herself. She got the bread knife out of the drawer, thanking God that Glynis had tied her hands in front of her instead of at the back and hopped to a chair, wedging the knife between her knees.

The sawing through took some time. The knife kept slipping against the pressure she was putting on it. Once her hands were free however it took only a moment to slash through the cord around her ankles. Walking took longer. She suffered with agonizing cramp.

What was the time? Nearly three. There had to be news of Jason by now.

She needed a pill . . . two pills. Her bag was gone. The gun of course. Glynis would have taken that. But where was everything else?

On the couch. Glynis had tipped everything out.

Her pills had rolled on to the floor. She swallowed two of the painkillers and stuffed everything back into her bag. The gun was the only thing Glynis had taken. As a precaution? Or did she plan on using it? Feeling a little uneasy at that thought and thinking of the way she had been stowed away out of sight Abby set off for the farm house and the phone.

She was only topping the first rise when she saw Glynis running along the path,

Denning at her heels. Neither of them had eyes to be looking much farther ahead than where their feet would next go and she got off the path quickly and buried herself in some gorse until they had gone past.

It wouldn't take them long to find out she'd gone. She started to run, the cliff path dancing dizzily in front of her. Flashes of the sheer drop at her left seemed to rush at her eyes. Her weak foot caught and turned over on a stone and she stumbled, staggering drunkenly to retain her balance.

She should have remained in the gorse. She'd have been safer there.

She glanced behind. Too late. They were both in pursuit. The path was a trap. There was no escape from it. Her breath was tortured now. She was sucking and gasping for air. So far to go yet. They were certain to catch up.

She topped another rise and down below saw a solitary figure trudging stolidly through the gorse. Mrs. Lloyd. There was no mistaking that determined battleship walk. Her relief was overwhelming. Hope provided fresh wings to her feet but the speed, combined with the steepness of the descent just there, sent her feet flying faster than she could cope with and she stumbled again.

This time there was no question of fighting for her balance. One second she was running, the next she was sliding over the edge of the path, the rocks below drawing her to them with a compelling certainty. Her hands closed desperately on an exposed root, her kicking feet steadied over an empty void and found some slight purchase and she screamed loudly for help.

Denning was the first to reach her. He stood at the edge of the path watching as the root she was clinging on to gradually succumbed to the pressure.

A spattering of earth hit Abby on the face and bounced off down into the void. She glanced down, then turned an agonized face up to him. He was going to watch her drop. He wasn't going to attempt to help. "Please . . ." she said faintly.

He made a slight movement and then Glynis was behind him. "No," she said harshly. "Let her drop. It's an accident, nothing to do with us."

"It will be murder." Mrs. Lloyd reached them. She was breathless but her voice, deep and much harsher than her daughter's, was compelling. "Get her up."

Denning reached down and caught her wrist just as the root gave up its last hold in the earth and came bursting free. She slipped down another couple of inches but Denning held her firmly, staggering only a little.

"Stand back," Mrs. Lloyd told Glynis firmly and helped Denning haul Abby up to the path.

She lay on her back, her eyes closed, gasping like a fish out of water.

"You don't know what you've done," Glynis said bitterly to her mother.

"Don't I? Didn't I warn you? And her too!"

Abby sat up. The deep grief underlying the harshness was like a rasp scraping on an open wound. This was no time to express any thanks to her for saving her life. She was looking at her as if she hated her. It was even worse than the way Glynis was looking at her.

"You'll come with me," Mrs. Lloyd said.

"No, she won't." Glynis faced her mother defiantly.

Two hard, implacable people, each with the same kind of strength. It was easy now to tell they were mother and daughter.

"It's no use. Can't you see that? You've lost almost everything. Retain what little you have left and let her go."

"No."

"You'll regret it."

"I don't think so."

Mrs. Lloyd nodded her head wearily. "Oh yes. You'll regret it. There's no way out for you now. Killing her will solve nothing. The police know everything."

"You said it was Wainwright she phoned. You said you were sure of it."

"It was the police who phoned back. They spoke to me. They've found your husband. They want you and they want this man here and they were very anxious about the girl."

"They've no proof of anything. Only her word for a conversation she overheard. That won't count for anything, especially if she's not around to repeat it."

"No," Denning said unexpectedly. "I'll not have any more killing. What happened was an accident. We can't undo that but we can stop ourselves going in deeper."

"I'm not giving myself up," Glynis said flatly. "No one is going to lock me up, ever."

"I'm having no part in any further killing," Denning said equally flatly.

There was a silence, broken by Mrs. Lloyd. "I've got some money. You could get away, change your names, leave the country."

"You've not got enough for me,"

Glynis said scornfully and then paused, "But Jason has, or he could raise it." She regarded Abby thoughtfully. "The old man would give the earth if he thought it meant saving your life." She raised her eyes to her mother. "Tell Jason. And tell the police to stay away from the cottage otherwise we start cutting her up piece by piece. Come on." She jerked Abby to her feet, twisting her arm behind her back. "Twenty thousand pounds," she called back to her mother. "That will do."

She pushed and prodded a stumbling Abby back to the cottage, Denning trailing behind in their wake.

His first action on getting in was to pour himself a stiff drink.

Glynis pushed Abby into a chair. "We'll have no trouble from you," she said grimly. "Howard! Keep an eye on her while I get some rope."

Abby sat apathetically in the chair. She didn't feel capable of making any kind of trouble. She was no match for Glynis alone, either in strength or agility. With the two of them she had no chance. Even if she managed to get out of the cottage there was still that long run to the farm. She couldn't hope to make it.

Glynis made sure of it. She tied her so tightly to the chair even Denning protested. "You'll stop her blood circulating."

"Who cares?" Glynis took another vicious pull at her knots.

"I should have given myself up right away," Denning said morosely. "I could have kept you out of it."

"It's too late for that now."

"Maybe not. I could say everything was my idea. I could take the blame for everything."

"With her around?"

"She's just come out of hospital. She had a brain operation didn't she? We could discount anything she said. She hates you. We could say she wasn't in her right mind."

"She won't be when I've finished with her certainly," Glynis said, baring her teeth in what would never have passed as a smile. "What can be a more pleasant way of passing the time than watching her squirm?"

"What do you mean?" Denning said uneasily.

"I mean that she's not going to come out of this laughing. In fact I wouldn't be surprised if she took all those pills she's got and put an end to her misery. Cat got your tongue?" she asked Abby. "Or did I do some damage to your vocal chords? It's not like you to keep quiet. Did you panic when you came round? Did you think you were in a coffin?"

Abby stared dully at her, not answering. Such a reaction didn't please Glynis. She slapped her smartly across the face two or three times. "When I speak to you, you answer."

"Leave her alone," Denning said, pouring himself another drink.

"Why should I? She's not going to end up with everything I worked for. That would be too much for me to bear. She's in love with Jason. Did you know that? She thinks he'll marry her. And she thinks she's going to get all the old man's money. How much do you think he's worth. Abigail? How much?" She slapped her again, hard, across the mouth. "Do you reckon twenty thousand is too little to ask for?"

"Will you stop it," Denning said angrily and pushed Glynis away from the chair. "Go and make something to eat if you want something to do."

"All right," Glynis said with a shrug. "I suppose I might as well."

Abby closed her eyes. There was blood in her mouth where her lip had caught against her teeth. Glynis clattered about in the kitchen, singing gaily as if she had nothing at all to worry about. Presently the smell of her cooking began to fill the cottage.

"Haven't you done anything for her?" Denning demanded as she brought out two plates and laid them on the table.

"Of course I have." Glynis opened her eyes wide. "A special offering."

"I don't want anything," Abby said quickly.

"You *can* talk then. I was beginning to

wonder." She came towards her with a dish in her hands. "Open wide."

Abby had no intention of doing any such thing. There was a gleam of joyful anticipation in Glynis's eyes.

"Come on. I don't want to be accused of starving you." She pinched her nose together, forcing her head back and as Abby gasped for air deftly filled her mouth. It was almost pure mustard with a little potato.

Abby choked, the tears starting from her eyes.

"Too hot for you?" Glynis said brightly. "Try a drink."

She poured salt water down, standing back with a smile as Abby retched and vomited, her body straining so violently that the chair overbalanced and she fell to the floor with an almighty crash.

"What *are* you doing?" Denning cried and came dashing over.

"I don't think she can face food," Glynis said blithely. "Something must have upset her stomach."

Denning straightened the chair and

regarded her grimly. "Try anything like that again and I'm turning her free. I won't stand for it."

"You won't stand for it!" Glynis said with a laugh. "And how are you going to stop me?"

He slapped her brutally across the face. "I can hand out treatment like that too. Stop plaguing her." He turned back to Abby, wiping her face with his handkerchief.

"Why don't you untie her while you're at it?" Glynis said in a deceptively casual voice.

"I think I will." Denning didn't turn round but Abby stiffened. She had a clear view of Glynis as he bent to pull at the knots and Glynis was holding a gun. *Her* gun.

She saw Denning's too. Tucked in his waistband. He released one hand and started on the other and feeling that she was rather taking an unfair advantage she leaned forward and plucked the gun out of his trousers.

"Sorry." She felt she had to apologize.

"But Glynis has a gun out and it's pointing at both of us. I have a funny feeling she's going to make you do something very unpleasant to me."

He flung a startled glance over his shoulder. "Glynis!"

"An interesting situation," Glynis said. "Do we count three and fire together?"

"Where did you get that gun? Glynis! Don't be silly!"

"Stay where you are," Glynis warned. "I wouldn't want to miss her."

"You'll miss," Abby said and managed to keep even the slightest tremor out of her voice. "Because Jason unloaded that gun when I fired it accidentally. He said it was too dangerous in my hands."

Glynis glanced down uncertainly and Denning jumped for her, making a snatch for the gun. It went off, shocking both into immobility. Denning recovered first and took the gun from Glynis's nerveless hand. "So it's not loaded," he said, glancing at Abby with a half smile. "I wondered if you were bluffing but you lie very convincingly."

"Didn't I tell you?" Glynis said bitterly. "Now what are you going to do?"

"I think Abigail is going to give my gun back to me," Denning said. "Aren't you?"

She met his eyes steadily. She was at a disadvantage she had no intention of disclosing. He obviously had no idea that his own gun was useless.

"I can take it from you very easily," Denning added. "But I don't want to hurt you."

"The more fool you." Glynis stood in front of Abby. "She'd never have the courage to shoot. Look at her face. Even if it meant saving her own life she couldn't do it. Hand it over, Abigail."

"I'll take it," Denning said.

"Oh no, you don't. You've got one. I'll have one too." She snatched it out of Abby's hand.

Denning sighed. "Very well. But put it away and let's have no more silly tricks."

"Okay." Glynis shrugged. "There's plenty of time for you to come round to my way of thinking." She put the gun in her bag and went back to the table.

Denning said to Abby, "Do you want something to eat?"

She shook her head emphatically.

"Some milk then?"

"If *you* get it."

He brought her a glass of milk which tasted like honey and nectar on her burning mouth.

"Tie that hand again," Glynis commanded.

"She's all right. She can't get out of that chair in a hurry." He picked up his plate and took it over to the window. "Do you think the police will come?"

"My mother will impress it on them that I meant business. If they've any thought for her safety they'll stay well away."

"There's no chance of Jason getting the money until tomorrow. Maybe not even then. It takes time to raise a sum like that. You realize that, don't you?"

"It doesn't matter. There's enough food here for weeks."

The afternoon dragged on. Glynis made no attempt to approach Abby again but her eyes rested on her frequently, the speculative gleam making her wonder uneasily what she had in mind for her next. She hoped Denning slept lightly. If Glynis got his gun she didn't like to think what might happen.

Dusk fell. Denning lit the lamps and drew the curtains. He had been drinking solidly throughout the afternoon, Glynis making no attempt to stop him, a sign which Abby found ominous.

"You know she'll ditch you at the first opportunity," she said abruptly as Denning opened a fresh bottle. "You've let her down and she doesn't need you any more."

"Shut up," Glynis said as Denning stared at her with a blank look on his face as if he'd not heard a word.

Abby ignored her. "Didn't it worry you when she turned that gun on you or was your concern wholly for me?"

"I'll shut it for you," Glynis said warningly.

"She's afraid you'll start thinking you see. Why aren't you planning what to do if you get the money? *If*, mind you. There's no guarantee that you'll get it and then what will you do? Even if you get it you can't simply vanish into thin air, can you?"

"We can go on using you," Glynis said shortly. "We can demand anything."

"But first you've got to get out of here. Think of that long stretch of nothing. A good marksman can lie in wait and get both of you before you even hear a shot."

"They wouldn't dare risk that."

"I don't see why not," Abby said pensively.

"We'll go in the dark."

"They'll still catch you. How many years will you get? You won't look so good when you come out, will you, Glynis? I reckon you'll be looking like your mother before long."

That hit home with a vengeance. Glynis got up and went into the kitchen without a word.

"She'll ditch you if it meant saving

herself," Abby said, persisting with Denning who still stared blankly at her. "Can't you see that? Your best plan is to give yourself up. You shouldn't listen to her."

He wasn't listening to anyone right then, certainly not to her. And Glynis came back and cut Abby's next words right off at the start by slapping a large piece of elastoplast across her mouth. Then she tied Abby's free hand back to the chair.

Denning jerked to attention at that. "What are you doing to her?"

"Nothing," Glynis said airily. "Merely making her secure for the night."

She brought another hard-backed chair up and straddled it, her arms resting on the back.

"You think I won't look so good," she said softly. "But how do you think you'll look when I've finished with you? Your teeth didn't get knocked out when those boys had a go at you, did they? What was it they did? A broken nose to start with? Will they be able to mend that if it gets smashed again? And those scars... Supposing they were ripped open again, with a tin opener perhaps, or the edge of a tin that's been open for days, all rusty and full of nasty germs..."

"What are you saying?" Denning said loudly. "What are you whispering for?"

"I didn't want to disturb you, darling. Why don't you go off to bed? You didn't get much sleep last night, remember?"

"I'm going to make some coffee," he said, lurching into the kitchen.

Glynis got up and closed the door. "It won't do him any good," she said. "You either." She opened Abby's bag and took out the sleeping pills. "I doped your drink the other night," she said casually, "They're not very strong, are they? How about six?" She smiled at Abby's horrified stare. "Too many? I don't think so." She swirled the liquid round, dropping the pills in one by one. "He'll never taste them. Not now. I despise people who can't hold their drink, don't you? It's so degrading. He's scared. That's why he's doing it. Scared rotten! Are you scared?

Maybe you don't believe I'd really hurt you? Maybe you think I'm bluffing? Just because I didn't kill you when I said I was going to. But I had second thoughts then. I'm not likely to have them now." She leaned forward, her eyes gleaming. "How about this for openers?"

She stretched out, holding her newly lit cigarette between her fingers, and was bringing it nearer and nearer to the flesh on the back of Abby's hand when Denning came back into the room and saw what she was doing.

His face went purple and he bounded forward and gave her a back-handed blow that sent her sprawling across the floor.

"I'm sorry," he said almost hysterically to Abby. "I'm sorry."

He picked up his drink and took a deep, gulping swallow.

Abby cried in her throat, shaking her head at him.

"Oh, for God's sake." He seemed to see the plaster for the first time and stretched out to take it off.

He'd barely touched it however when

Glynis launched herself forward and knocked his arm away. "Leave it, leave it."

"Why? I don't understand you, Glynis. What are you trying to do?"

"What are *you* trying to do? You're drunk. Look at you! Swaying and slobbering all over the place. Where's your common sense? Do you want to let her get away? Say goodbye to our money? Finish your drink, for God's sake, and get off to bed to sleep it off."

"You're going to hurt that girl," he said accusingly. "You don't like her. You said so . . . said you'd never liked her. She's coming with me. I'll look after you," he said owlishly to Abby. "You see. You come to bed now." He swayed and took another swallow.

Abby closed her eyes in despair. Six pills. On top of all that alcohol.

"I'll get a knife," Denning said thickly. "Set you free."

This time Glynis made no attempt to stop him. She watched him reel into the kitchen and reel back, brandishing a big butcher's knife. She was smiling. "I rather think this is where you'll be losing your first blood," she commented in amusement and sat down on the couch for a grandstand view.

Abby was inclined to share her opinion. Denning stood in front of her, trying hard to focus. The knife meandered through the air and he looked at it, squinting. "Too big," he muttered.

"Maybe this one will be better," Jason said from the kitchen doorway. He was in slacks and a polo necked sweater, both black, and his face and hands were grimy and dirt covered. He had a knife in his hands, a slim stiletto, and the lamp light seemed to pick on the blade and then reflect on his teeth as he smiled.

Denning didn't move. That is to say he didn't make any antagonistic move, remaining swaying on his feet, and blinking at Jason.

"Why didn't you knock?" Glynis said coolly. "There was no need at all to climb in through the window. Were you told about the money? Twenty thousand pounds?"

"I'm afraid I've not got it with me," he said apologetically. "I always insist on examining the goods before I do business. Take that plaster off her mouth. I want to ask her if she is all right."

"Of course she's all right. Would I harm my investment? No . . . stay where you are." She dived into her bag and produced Denning's gun. "When can you get the money?"

"If you've harmed one hair of her head," Jason said deliberately. "You won't live to enjoy a penny of it."

"I've not touched her. It was him. Look at him now . . . with that knife. I couldn't stop him."

"S'lie," Denning said thickly. "S'lie. I was cutting her free." He brought the knife up and by some miraculous luck severed through one strand around the arm of the chair. He stared at it, blinking. "Bloody marvellous. Bloo—dy marvellous," and brought his hand up in another swing. He missed by a yard this time, the impetus spinning him round. For a moment it seemed as if he would do a complete spiral and then his legs folded up beneath him and he fell on his back and commenced to snore lustily.

"A fine partner you picked," Jason commented without expression.

"I had no choice. It was an accident, Jason. You do believe that, don't you? Nothing was planned."

"What about my suicide?"

"It was a way out. It was all I could think of. I didn't want to do it. If I could have put Howard in your place I would have done."

"What stopped you?" He leaned against the door, the slender blade glinting as he turned it around in his hand.

Abby pulled at the severed bonds, loosening them. She could free that hand, slide it out and work on the other, but Glynis was too near. She would see her. She watched Jason, willing him to distract Glynis's attention.

"Would you have killed for me?" Glynis asked in a low voice.

"I'd have considered it."

Glynis thought that over and then stood up. "You could get that money," she said. "And we could go away, together. You and I."

She moved forward, and in doing so presented her back to Abby.

Abby feverishly pulled her hand free and tugged at the knots on the other side.

"South America," Jason suggested. "I have contacts. I could get you away."

"Maybe you could make it thirty thousand? He'd give anything, wouldn't he?"

"I believe he would."

The last knot yielded. She bent to untie her feet.

"You only wanted her because of the money, didn't you?" Glynis asked with a hint of a plea in her voice. "You didn't love her."

"How could I? With you around? There's never been anyone else but you, Glynis. No one can match you. You're beautiful. The only woman I've ever loved."

Glynis stopped her approach to him, keeping her distance, but she said. "I used to believe that but you made me wonder this weekend. She was so sure of herself."

Abby pulled the plaster off her mouth, taking the harshest way, but the quickest. It made a ripping snap and Glynis turned quickly at the sound.

"Her gun's not loaded," Abby told Jason pleasantly. "Of course if you wish to continue your scintillating conversation you may do so."

"It won't work a second time," Glynis said scornfully. "What do you take me for?"

"A complete moron in some respects. Lapping all that up! I suppose he knew that was one certain way of getting your complete attention."

"Could you see what she was doing?" Glynis whirled back on Jason and saw the answer from the faint amusement on his face. She backed against the wall where she could keep both of them within her range of vision. "I'll not kill her," she said in a biting, deadly voice. "Rest assured of that. But I'll make her wish she was dead. You get that money as fast as you can for the longer you linger the more she'll suffer."

"She likes to talk that way," Abby said kindly. "It gives her illusions of grandeur."

"How would you like your ear nicked?" Glynis said savagely. She walked towards Abby and held the gun close to her head. "Get going or I'll do it," she told Jason.

"The bullets for that gun are down in a sewer in Cardiff," Abby said and even as the words left her mouth she wondered if Denning had discovered what she had done and reloaded.

"Stand away from her," Jason said softly. "I don't want to kill you, Glynis."

"Kill me! I'm the one with the gun in this room."

"Oh, but you forget this." He stroked the blade of the knife lovingly.

Glynis laughed. "What can you do with that? Throw it? From that distance?"

"Certainly from that distance."

"Stop me then." She smiled triumphantly and pulled the trigger.

Abby had flung herself forward and was sprawling across Denning's body, fumbling for the gun in his waistband before she registered that the noise in her ear had been only a click instead of a loud bang.

She turned on her side awkwardly. After so long in the chair she could hardly move and she felt as if she had been moulded into a sitting position.

Her jaw dropped as she stared at Glynis. The gun had dropped from her fingers and she had a hand to her shoulder where the hilt of the knife protruded. Blood trickled over the fingers which crept wonderingly around the shaft. "Jason!" she whispered, incredulous and disbelieving.

He walked forward slowly, his lips twisting. "I'm sorry, Glynis, but I did warn you. You could hardly expect me to let you get away with it. Don't worry. You're not going to die."

"But Jason . . . I—" She swayed and he caught her in his arms and carried her over to the couch.

Abby turned her eyes away and slowly and painfully got to her feet.

The cramp was appalling. She had to bite her lips to keep from screaming.

"Are the police near by?" she asked quietly.

"Open the door." Jason was putting a pad on Glynis's shoulder and he didn't look up.

Abby opened the door and looked straight into the grim visage of Foster.

"You're all right, lass?" he said, shouldering his way past her. "That's good. Tell me what happened."

In a few minutes it seemed the cottage was milling with policemen of all shapes and sizes, in uniform and out of it. Abby told her story, Jason added a few words, both Denning and Glynis were carried off bound for the hospital and then all of a sudden she was alone with Jason.

"What will happen to her?" Abby asked.

"She'll stand trial with Denning and she'll go to prison." Jason sounded weary.

"I told you it wasn't loaded," Abby said. "You needn't have done that to her. You might . . . you might have killed her."

"I couldn't take a chance," Jason said. "I think she was a little mad. All her planning gone astray because of you. I was afraid."

Abby went to the window. A slow procession was winding its way up the cliff path, the many torches dotting the darkness like fireflies.

"They took my gun," she mourned.

"You'll not need it. Tomorrow we're off to Jamaica. No one is going to look for you there."

"Jamaica," she said pensively without looking around.

"It's a nice place to relax and get a tan and enjoy the scenery. I've got a job to do there."

"What kind of a job?"

"Wrecking a beautiful piece of machinery in the most spectacular way possible."

"Is it—is it against the law?"

He shook his head in amusement. "I'm no crook, Abigail. Sorry to disappoint you. I merely work in the movie industry. It's well paid but erratic and there are times when I live high and others when I barely exist. I've never saved a penny and no insurance company would give me cover. I'm what's known as a stunt man. I crash cars and motor bikes and fall down stairs and jump from moving vehicles. You'll have seen the kind of thing. They can't risk any of the stars having an accident. It's bad economics."

"Has your father told you to take me with you?"

He got up and went over to her, turning her around with his forefinger on her chin. Tilting her head back so that she met his eyes he said, "Now when did my father last tell me to do anything? He doesn't know yet. We'll see him tomorrow before we go."

"Does he know anything?"

"I couldn't tell him . . . not until it was all over. What would I have told him when he asked where you were?" He smiled at her. "I'd have been disowned immediately for leaving you here alone."

"You were hoping all the time, weren't you? Hoping that I was wrong?"

The smile vanished abruptly and he dropped his hand. It was regrettable but it had to be faced. Once only. And then she would never refer to it again. "Would you have killed for her?"

"No," he said. "I wouldn't have done that."

She stared at his bleak face and felt a shiver go down her back. Not that. What then? To what lengths would he have gone. No more. She didn't want to know. Let it die and wither with time. "I'll make you forget her," she stated flatly. "I can do it."

He regarded her gravely for a long moment and then reached behind her and pulled the curtains tightly together, dropping his hands on her shoulders. "I should leave you at my father's," he said. "I should leave you and tell him to guard you close and keep you well away from me because there are going to be times when you'll be hurt. I'm the last person you should have fallen in love with. You're too young, too trusting, too vulnerable. And I am . . . what I am."

"But you're not going to leave me."

"No." He smiled crookedly. "I'm not. That's a pointer for you. I'm selfish along with all my other faults. Right now I want you with me, all the time. You'll keep my nightmares at bay. Tomorrow it might be different but until then you're not having any say in the matter. You're coming."

"Don't you know tomorrow never comes," Abby said softly. "And you shouldn't assume too many things. I'm not all that young and I'm not at all trusting besides being very hardboiled indeed. And what makes you think I'm in love with you?"

"Aren't you?"

She hesitated. One didn't go around admitting something like that. Not unless

... Unless ... She smiled a little. She was half-way there. "I guess I must be. You're not frightening me at all. There's just one thing worrying me. Are you going to go on calling me Abigail? Only I've grown to positively hate that name."

"Didn't I tell you! You don't suit it a bit. What do you want? Diana or Sibyl or—"

"Abby will do," she said firmly.

He shook his head, his eyes laughing again. "I think she will. Yes indeed! She'll do." And he let his hands drop from her shoulders and drew her close.

THE END

*Books by Margaret Carr
in the Linford Mystery Library:*

DAGGERS DRAWN
BLINDMAN'S BLUFF
SHARENDEL
TWIN TRAGEDY
WHO'S THE TARGET?

*Other titles in the
Linford Western Library:*

FARGO: MASSACRE RIVER
by John Benteen

Fargo spurred his horse to the edge of the road. The ambushers up ahead had now blocked the road. Fargo's convoy was a jumble, a perfect target for the insurgents' weapons!

SUNDANCE: DEATH IN THE LAVA
by John Benteen

The land echoed with the thundering hoofs of Modoc ponies. In minutes they swooped down and captured the wagon train and its cargo of gold. But now the halfbreed they called Sundance was going after it, and he swore nothing would stand in his way.

GUNS OF FURY
by Ernest Haycox

Dane Starr, alias Dan Smith, wanted to close the door on his past and hang up his guns, but people wouldn't let him. Good men wanted him to settle their scores for them. Bad men thought they were faster and itched to prove it. Starr had to keep killing just to stay alive.

FARGO: PANAMA GOLD
by John Benteen

Cleve Buckner was recruiting an army of killers, gunmen and deserters from all over Central America. With foreign money behind him, Buckner was going to destroy the Panama Canal before it could be completed. Fargo's job was to stop Buckner—and to eliminate him once and for all!

FARGO: THE SHARPSHOOTERS
by John Benteen

The Canfield clan, thirty strong, were raising hell in Texas. One of them had shot a Texas Ranger, and the Rangers had to bring in the killer. Fargo was tough enough to hold his own against the whole clan.

SUNDANCE: OVERKILL
by John Benteen

Sundance's reputation as a fighting man had spread. There was no job too tough for the halfbreed to handle. So when a wealthy banker's daughter was kidnapped by the Cheyenne, he offered Sundance $10,000 to rescue the girl.

HELL RIDERS
by Steve Mensing
Wade Walker's kid brother, Duane, was locked up in the Silver City jail facing a rope at dawn. Wade was a ruthless outlaw, but he was smart, and he had vowed to have his brother out of jail before morning!

DESERT OF THE DAMNED
by Nelson Nye
The law was after him for the murder of a marshal—a murder he didn't commit. Breen was after him for revenge—and Breen wouldn't stop at anything . . . blackmail, a frameup . . . or murder.

DAY OF THE COMANCHEROS
by Steven C. Lawrence
Their very name struck terror into men's hearts—the Comancheros, a savage army of cutthroats who swept across Texas, leaving behind a bloodstained trail of robbery and murder.